BACKSTAGE NIGHT WITH THE BILLIONAIRE

MARIAH ANKENMAN

Harlequin ROMANCE

Recycling programs for this product may not exist in your area.

ISBN-13: 978-1-335-47085-0

Backstage Night with the Billionaire

For questions and comments about the quality of this book, please contact us at CustomerService@Harlequin.com.

Harlequin Enterprises ULC
22 Adelaide St. West, 41st Floor
Toronto, Ontario M5H 4E3, Canada
www.Harlequin.com

HarperCollins Publishers
Macken House, 39/40 Mayor Street Upper,
Dublin 1, D01 C9W8, Ireland
www.HarperCollins.com

Printed in U.S.A.

1 2 3 4 5 6 7 8 9 10 HDC 28 27 26 25

A brand-new trilogy from Harleqiun Romance author Mariah Ankenman.

Love Under Construction

Caution: Cupid at work!

In a fix? Call the Thorsons! Billionaire brothers Kell, Cash and Mal build dream castles for the elite—the sky's the limit on what they can achieve for their über-wealthy clientele. And yet their real passion project is their charity, Helping Hands, where they fix up homes for those in need. Running a real estate empire *and* doing good doesn't leave much time for any distractions—which is why *none* of them are looking for love.

But no hard hat can protect you from contracting feelings... Kell, Cash and Mal are about to learn that to find forever, sometimes you have to throw away the blueprints and follow your heart!

Read Kell and Piper's story in

Backstage Night with the Billionaire

Available now!

And look out for Cash's and Mal's stories,

Both coming soon!

Dear Reader,

Have you ever seen an aerial dance show and thought, *Wow, that looks fun?* Writing an aerialist heroine was so exciting, as I got to draw on my own experience as an aerialist. The thing I love most about aerials is how versatile it is. With all the different apparatuses, it can be modified for any body and ability. I knew sweet and caring Piper was the perfect person to run an aerial studio. As this story came to me, I had to pair my romantic aerial performer with a realist who prefers his feet on the ground. Piper and Kell are opposites in almost every way, but you know what they say about opposites attracting. These two couldn't be more different, but the more time they spend together, the more they realize your perfect person might be the very last one you ever imagined.

Mariah Ankenman

Bestselling author **Mariah Ankenman** lives in the beautiful Rocky Mountains with her two rambunctious children and loving spouse, who is her own personal spell-checker when her dyslexia gets the best of her. Mariah loves to lose herself in a world of words. Her favorite thing about writing is when she can make someone's day a little brighter with one of her books. To learn more about Mariah and her books, visit her website, mariahankenman.com, follow her on social media or sign up for her newsletter.

Books by Mariah Ankenman

Harlequin Romance

Accidentally Dating the Enemy
Cinderella's Bargain with the Billionaire

Visit the Author Profile page at Harlequin.com.

To aerials. Here's to dancing in the sky
and only breaking one bone...so far.

CHAPTER ONE

WAKING UP TO a drip of nasty roof water wasn't the best way to greet the day, but thanks to the leak in her ceiling today, that was exactly how Piper Pitts woke up.

"Ew!" she exclaimed, tossing her covers off and jumping up from the cot currently serving as her bed. "Oh, come on! It's not even seven a.m.!"

Life was really taking a cue from her last name these days. Every time she thought she'd hit the bottom, something came along to prove her wrong. She glared up at the ceiling where a small, discolored spot was slowly dripping brownish droplets of water. What were the odds that the roof would leak in the exact spot where she laid her head to rest?

"The way my life is going, a hundred percent," she grumbled into the small storage room she'd turned into a makeshift bedroom.

Grabbing the cot, she pulled it away from the dripping water. She'd need to grab a bucket from the basement to catch the water until she could figure out how to fix the leak. Not like she could count on her landlord to fix it. This leak would be item number sixty-seven on her repair list. The repair list she'd been sending him for months, that he kept saying he'd "get around to" but never did. Donald was useless. The only time he ever responded to her was if she asked for a rent extension. And then it was with a resounding "no."

"Jerk," she muttered.

Picking up the empty plastic bowl she'd eaten her take-out dinner salad from last night, she placed it under the leak.

"There." She smiled, nodding approvingly at her own quick thinking. "This will work until I can grab a bucket. Then all I have to do is look up a roof patching tutorial online and it will be smooth sailing."

For this problem at least. The other sixty-six issues were…less easy to fix. She rented the whole theater—complete with rehearsal spaces—and all of it was falling apart. Loose floorboards here, broken toilets there, and several other issues her landlord should be fixing but wasn't. Another person might hire legal help to force Donald to fulfil his obligations. But Piper was underwater in the funds department right now.

Plus, there was the small issue of her living at the theater in secret. If Donald discovered she was living here…he'd have means to break her lease and kick her out. There went her aerial studio and all the amazing artists who rented out the theater for their performances.

She could not let that happen. It had taken years of saving, a successful crowdfunding campaign and a loan she'd be paying off until she died for her to secure the deposit to rent this place in the first place, and to buy all the equipment she needed. Who knew how long it would take her to repeat that process if she had to find another place? Years probably, and by then she'd have lost all her students.

Besides, living here was only temporary.

"Extenuating circumstances." She sighed, remembering how her ex had lied to her, cleaned out their joint bank account and disappeared into the night four months ago. Leaving her with a lease she couldn't pay, which had resulted in her getting kicked out of her apartment. "And here I am."

She stared at the leak, wondering when exactly her life had gotten so complicated.

The life of an artist is a sad and poor one, Piper. I'm not paying for some silly circus school. You'll get a sensible accounting degree like I did or you're on your own.

Her father's words rang in her memory, the sharp sting of his conditional love still hurting even ten years later.

"Stop moping, Piper," she said to herself. "Put on your big girl panties. There's a lot of work to do and if you want to succeed you can only count on yourself."

Affirmation in place, she quickly dressed. As

she grabbed a hairbrush to tackle her bed head, a noise from downstairs made her freeze. No one should be in the theater right now. There were no classes today and no performances scheduled until next month. Her heart raced in her chest as she listened, hoping it was just her imagination.

The distinct sound of shoes walking across the stage floor had her hopes dashed and her fear skyrocketing.

Eyes searching her room, she looked for her cell to call the police. She spied it on the floor next to her planner, cursing when she saw the black screen and realized she forgot to plug it in last night.

"Dammit, Piper!"

She moved to the door and carefully cracked it open. Maybe one of her students had gotten their days mixed up and thought there was class today? No. She'd locked the doors last night. How would they have gotten in?

She glanced down to see a tall white man with dark hair standing in the middle of the stage. His back was to her so she couldn't see his face, but he was wearing slacks and a flannel shirt. Was she being robbed by a lumberjack?

Quietly stepping out of her room, she tiptoed down the small set of stairs that led from the upper storage room to the back of the stage. As she moved, she spied a bat from the children's production that had been performed here over the summer. She grabbed the makeshift weapon in her hands and gripped it tight. The red plastic child's toy wasn't the best option against a burglar, but it was all she had.

As the man kept his back to her, she silently crept up behind him. He was tall, at least a foot taller than her, but she was strong from her aerial training. Lifting the bat high above her head, she brought it down on his back with as much force as possible as she screamed, "Get out of my theater!"

The man let out a startled yelp and turned.

Fear paused for a split second as Piper took in her intruder's face. Holy handsome, Batman!

Her jaw dropped open as the most beautifully piercing blue eyes she'd ever seen stared back at her with confusion and shock. Said eyes glanced at the bat and back to her. One hand reached up to rub the shoulder she'd hit as he opened his mouth and a deep, rich voice emerged.

"Did you just hit me with a Wiffle Ball bat?"

Her eyes darted to the bat and back to him. "Yes."

"Why?"

She scoffed. He broke into her place and had the audacity to question her defense tactics?

"Why are you in my theater?" she countered. "There's nothing here to steal. Haven't you heard the term *starving artist*? We got nothing, Jack."

"Kellen."

She frowned. "Huh?"

"My name. It's Kellen. Not Jack. But my friends call me Kell."

Weirdest. Robber. Ever.

"Okay…Kellen. I'll ask again. Why are you in my theater?" She lifted the bat again, preparing to strike once more.

"Woah." He raised his hands in surrender. "Put the bat down, ma'am. I'm not here to steal anything, I promise you. I'm here to do repairs."

She frowned, lowering the bat…slightly. "Repairs?"

He nodded. "Mr. Donald Noll hired me to complete repairs at the Star-Crossed Theater. This is the place, correct?"

Her brain started firing, catching up as his words sunk in. Donald had finally hired someone to fix all the issues she'd been complaining about. *Or so he says...*

She lifted the bat again, grip tightening. "Prove it."

"Excuse me?"

"Prove that my landlord hired you to do repairs. Because I've been asking for months and not a single contractor has reached out. Then suddenly here you are in the wee hours of the morning, somehow in my theater which was locked, claiming to be the repairman."

A small smile ticked up the corner of his mouth. A mouth she refused to think of as sexy…even if it was.

"I apologize for scaring you," he said, lifting a clipboard. "Here is the paperwork Mr. Noll sent me. He also gave me a key to the place, which is how I got in. He told me no one would be here this morning. Otherwise, I would have announced my presence."

Right. Of course Donald thought no one would be here. He didn't know Piper was squatting.

"I, um, came in to do some…repairs. Since Mr. Noll refuses to fix anything around here." There. That sounded like a reasonable explanation. Not that she needed to explain herself to this man. But just in case he relayed this interaction to Donald, she wanted her ducks in a row. After all, he might say he was here to fix things, but she wouldn't put it past Donald to send some creep to spy on her. Catch her doing something against her lease so he could kick her out.

Something like squatting…

Her defenses rose. She needed to play this smart. No trusting this guy, no matter how unfairly attractive he was.

"That refusal has come to an end," Kellen said, still holding out the clipboard.

Keeping her guard up, she held the bat in one hand while reaching out for the clipboard. He didn't appear to be dangerous. Honestly, he looked like a guy who would have a TV show called *The Handsome Handyman.* Nothing about him seemed threatening. He didn't even have a toolbox, which was kind of suspicious, considering he claimed to be a contractor.

She glanced down at the clipboard to see some paperwork. It looked like a work order of some kind. Donald's name and signature was on there, along with jargon relating to building repairs. A sigh of relief filled her as she finally felt safe enough to lower the bat. Donald indeed hired him.

He could still be a spy, a voice whispered in the back of her mind. Relieved that he wasn't a robber, but suspicion still swirling in her brain, she nodded.

"It's about freaking time," she said, handing the clipboard back.

Kell took it with a puzzled expression. "You said these repairs have been needed for months?"

She nodded. "Some for months, some for weeks. They keep piling up."

Kell glanced at the paperwork. "It is a rather long list."

"Wouldn't have been this long if he would have fixed stuff as it broke. When I told him about it."

A small chuckle left his lips. "Yes, well, as you said, *starving artist* is a common phrase but so is *scummy landlord*." He winked. "Don't tell him I said that."

She chuckled along with him, anxiety easing. "I won't. If you promise not to tell anyone about the…" She lifted the bat.

He graced her with a smile that had her heart

skipping several beats. Good grief, this man was handsome.

"My lips are sealed." He rolled his shoulders. "Though my back might be sore for a few days."

Guilt sneaking in, she took a step forward. "Shoot, I'm sorry. Did I hurt you? I really thought you were trying to rob me or..." She let her words trail off, not revealing the bleaker thoughts that had crept into her mind when she saw a strange man standing on the darkened stage.

His jovial smile slipped. True remorse and concern filled his eyes as he stared at her.

"I would never fault anyone for defending themselves. I truly apologize for scaring you. I swear I had no idea anyone would be here. Mr. Noll said the place would be empty and I would have free rein to do whatever I needed."

She snorted. "Sounds like something he would say. Why would he need to inform me, his tenant, about a repairman coming in? Leave it up to the boys."

Not only was Donald a scummy landlord, but he was also a sexist jerk.

"Would you like me to come back later?" Kell asked. "Is there a time that works better for you?"

He was asking her? That was a new one. The very, very few times Donald had sent someone in to fix things, the contractors never cared about her schedule. They could be in the middle of dress rehearsal, aerial silks hanging from the rafters and

Joe Schmoe Blow would stomp all over her stage claiming he needed to get to the furnace room now. She wasn't used to consideration from people Donald hired.

Too good to be true! the voice screamed. *He's up to something.*

Tucking her suspicions away to examine later, she masked her emotions and put on her service-worker smile.

"Now works," she said. "Today is actually perfect. There are no classes, so the place is empty."

He smiled, making her heart race again. This was ridiculous. She was in the arts. Over the years in her career, she'd worked with some of the most beautiful people on the planet. Why was this guy making her heart pitter-patter like a schoolgirl with a crush? Must be the adrenaline from thinking he was here to hurt her. That was all. Leftover endorphins confused for attraction.

"Would you care to show me around?" Kell asked. "If you're not busy, that is. I have the list from Mr. Noll, but I have a feeling you can show me what's needed better than any list."

She sure could. In fact, she'd bet the last dollar she had a lot of the repairs needed weren't even on the list Donald gave him.

"I am happy to show you around, Kellen."

"Call me Kell, please. And you are?"

Sticking out her hand, she smiled. "Piper."

"It's nice to meet you, Piper."

He grasped her hand in his and shook. A spark of heat filled her palm at his touch, warming her entire body until her toes tingled. She quickly pulled her hand back, avoiding looking at him as she glanced at the bat still in her other hand.

"Not sure bashing you with a plastic bat is what most people would consider nice. I think most people would call it strange."

He shrugged. "It's a unique introduction. Can't argue with that. And what's wrong with being strange?"

A lot, according to every person who had ever bullied Piper for being the weird kid. Took until highschool and a yearlong waitlist to finally realize her "weirdness" was not a personality fault, but in fact autism. Not that her bullies had cared.

"Shall we?" he asked, indicating the back of the stage with his hand.

"Follow me," she said, turning, her cheeks heating as this man's gentlemanly charm once again set her off-kilter.

While her body heated like a coed on spring break, her mind reminded her that this man was sent from her enemy. He might say he was there to help, but she'd learned long ago that casual lying was common amongst most people. She couldn't let her guard down in case he was here as a spy for Donald. She'd been wrong about people too many times. Her best friend always said she was too trusting. Now more than ever was the time for caution. No matter how handsome Kell was, he could have nefarious intent. She had to discover if he was here for more than just building repairs, and if he was…she was in trouble.

CHAPTER TWO

KELL HADN'T BEEN hit with a Wiffle Ball bat since he was a kid. Then the attacker had usually been one of his brothers, Cash or Mal, not really an experience comparable to his meeting with the small, beautiful woman currently leading him across the empty stage. Kell felt terrible for scaring her. Damn Donald for not warning him someone might be in the theater. The guy had told Kell the place would be empty. He had also said the current tenant was a nightmarish nagging shrew.

Piper was as far from a nightmare as one could get.

The petite white woman couldn't be more than five feet tall, but she had the fierceness of a titan—and the strength, judging by the way Kell's shoulder still throbbed. His brothers' hits never hurt this much. Watching her walk ahead of him, he could see the muscles in her upper arms bared by the straps of the dark blue tank top she wore. Donald had said something about her being a dancer. Kell had known a few dancers over the years. Their workout routines were intense.

"We'll head to the basement first," Piper said, glancing at him over her shoulder. "That's where the big issues are."

He nodded. "Sounds like a plan."

She smiled, taking his breath away with the way her smile lit up the entire room. Not an easy feat, considering they were at the edge of the very large empty theater. Definitely not a shrew.

Piper was beautiful. Her pale skin was dusted with light brown freckles hidden among the vibrant multicolored flower tattoos cascading down both arms. Her dark brown hair was wavy and slightly tousled, like she'd just gotten out of bed.

He spied streaks of dark blue among the strands. Blue had always been his favorite color.

"Watch the second step. The board is loose and moves on you a bit." She pointed to the second stair of the steps leading down to the basement before carefully stepping on the right edge of it. He brought his clipboard up, making a note about the stairs on the paper. That issue had not been mentioned by Donald. Not surprising. A lot of landlords had no idea of all the issues in their properties that needed fixing.

Handyman work wasn't Kell's normal job. He and his brothers ran Thorson Realty, one of the most successful real estate agencies in the Denver Metro area and beyond. They catered to the wealthy, the elite. Snobs.

One might say Kell himself was in that category, but while he and his brothers did very well for themselves, they didn't exactly *enjoy* the trappings and pretentiousness of high society. Which was why they also headed up the Helping Homes division of the Thorson Foundation, a charity with many branches started by their late aunt and uncle and currently run by their cousin, Rory Thorson. Kell and his brothers repaired abandoned and foreclosed homes and donated them to those in need.

Along with his real estate license, Kell had licenses in nearly every area of contract work from electrical to plumbing to roofing. He was a jack-of-all-trades. In the housing market, that was.

"I think the electrics should be your first priority," Piper said as they reached the basement landing. She moved over to the far wall where the fuse box hung.

He made his way over to her, squinting in the darkness. The only light came from a small high window on the opposite wall. The musty smell of dirt surrounded him. Standard basement smell. He breathed a sigh of relief at the lack of rotten eggs. Old buildings like this were notorious for gas leaks. He could fix a lot of things, but a gas leak called for the real professionals.

"Is there an overhead light we could turn on?"

Piper snorted. "Yeah, but it won't do much good considering it burned out weeks ago. Before you ask, it's not the bulb. I replaced the bulb, and it still doesn't work."

He turned to look at her in the dim light. "I'm assuming you told Mr. Noll about this?"

She rolled her dark brown eyes and let out a heavy sigh. "I did and he told me I must not know how to screw in a light bulb properly."

Wow, *jerk* was too nice a word for the guy. Kell couldn't say he had much cared for the man when he met him. Donald was rude, self-important, and never stopped talking. But a paycheck was a paycheck, and this one would be a gold mine for him and his brothers, which would mean extra funds for Helping Homes. He'd gladly take money from a tactless buffoon and use it to help those who deserved it.

Only…

"I swear the man thinks I don't have a brain cell because I have boobs." Her cheeks flushed a pretty pink as the words left her mouth. Her arms crossed over her chest. Clearing her throat, she ducked her head. "What I mean is, he's kind of a misogynist."

He nodded, doing his best to focus on grabbing the flashlight attached to his belt. He hid a smile as he pulled the tool free. Her tendency to speak what was on her mind without filtering it was refreshing and charming.

"Can't say I've known the man long, but based on our limited interactions I have to agree with you." He grinned over at her. "Again, don't tell him I said that."

She mimed zipping her lips and throwing away

the key. He laughed, utterly delighted by this woman who only minutes ago had been bashing him with a plastic bat. She might call it strange, but he considered it an unforgettable introduction.

"Now," he said, focusing on the box in front of him. "Let's take a look and see what we've got."

He opened the metal fuse box, coughing slightly as a layer of dust kicked up with the movement. When was the last time Donald had someone down here to inspect things? The landlord was in for a rude awakening if he thought he could just slap a few coats of paint on this place and call it good. One look at the inside and Kell knew he was in for a hard job.

"How long have you been Mr. Noll's tenant?"

"I've been renting the theater for over three years now. It'll be four in six weeks, when the lease renewal happens."

He swallowed down a hefty dose of guilt.

This was the second time Piper had mentioned her lease renewal. The second time he'd had to hold his tongue. Because he knew something she clearly didn't. Something good old Donald must not have informed his tenant of. The reason Kell had been hired.

Yes, he was here to fix the place up thanks to his contractor licensing, but the main point of his contract with Donald Noll was to sell the place. Places like this were in high demand. Due to the historical nature of the building, it couldn't be torn down so they'd be looking for buyers who required a theater space. Not a huge market, but Kell already had a few leads from his high society acquaintances who were looking for unique spaces to host their galas and other functions.

Donald claimed he was tired of the hassle of being a landlord. What a joke. Judging by the state of this place, he'd bet the guy hadn't stepped one foot in it since renting it to Piper. He clearly hadn't been keeping up with proper maintenance. A property like this, with its historical nature and location in the heart of the city, would fetch a large profit. Even in the current market. Kell was set to make a pretty penny from the repairs and even more from the sale. As much as it made his stomach sour to keep news of the impending sale from Piper, legally he couldn't say a word.

The thing about contracts was that they were there to protect both parties. In this case, his contract with Donald had specific language stating he was not to inform the current tenant of his plan to put the property on the market in six weeks. Piper's lease would expire, and she'd be out. Awful, but legally Donald wasn't doing anything wrong. Morally…that was an entirely different story.

Kell glanced over to Piper, guilt burning his chest as he swallowed down the terrible information he held. It wasn't like he knew this woman well, wasn't friends with her. He had no obligation to tell her her landlord was scum. Hell, she knew that. She didn't know he was planning on kicking her out, but unfortunately, Kell couldn't tell her.

If he did, he'd not only lose his contract, but it would open him up to a lawsuit; he could lose his licenses, and that could impact Helping Homes. He couldn't risk it.

"Has anyone come out in that time and done any repairs?" he asked, pushing his guilt down as he focused on the task at hand.

She frowned, face scrunching as she concentrated. "We had a plumber come out when the backstage bathroom toilets backed up. That was about a year ago. I can't remember anyone else coming for anything recently."

He swallowed down the rising rage. "No one? Not an HVAC tech or electrician?"

Many appliances required yearly maintenance. As the landlord, Donald was responsible to see to these things.

Piper shook her head. "Donald always told me he had someone come out to check things when I wasn't here, but I don't believe him."

Looking at the state of this fuse box, Kell didn't either.

"Well, I can't tell you exactly why the basement light isn't working, but I can assure you it's not because of your light bulb replacing skills. Which I'm sure are top-notch."

She laughed. "Oh yes, I'm the best light bulb replacer in the whole metro area. Ask anyone. I've won awards."

He chuckled along with her, charmed by her peculiar sense of humor.

He made a note on his clipboard, flashing his light around the basement when he finished. "You were right. Electrics will take top priority. Anything else down here need fixing?"

She leaned forward, glancing at his clipboard with a concerned expression. "How many things did Donald say needed fixing?"

"I have thirteen items to be fixed on my list."

"Ha!" Piper threw her head back and let out a sardonic bark of laughter. "Maybe it would have been thirteen two years ago. I swear that man just sends my emails to spam."

Unease crept into his gut. "How many emails have you sent?"

"About the repairs needed?" Her eyebrows rose as she lifted her hands and silently counted off on her fingers. "Over fifty."

Fifty! His blood boiled again at Donald's negligence.

"But some of those fixes were easy enough for me to do and some new things have popped up." She sighed. "I'm sorry to say this job is gonna be bigger than you planned for."

He was coming to realize that. In more ways than one. He took a quick breath to center himself and shove his true emotions about this situation deep down inside. Pasting on his friendly client smile, he shrugged. “I’m always up for a challenge.”

She smiled back, a genuine one that nearly knocked him off his feet. Her smile warmed the cold, dank air around them, causing something in his chest to tighten.

“You, Kell, are my hero.”

His smile dipped at her joy-filled words. Shame weighed heavy on his shoulders. Piper might think he was her hero, there to fix all her problems and leave her with a fully functional business space, but in reality, he was her executioner. Here to crush her dreams as he helped take away a space she clearly loved.

This was a nightmare.

CHAPTER THREE

FINALLY, IT WAS HAPPENING!

Piper took the first breath of relief in months. Kell was a literal angel. Donald might be a scumbag of the biggest degree, but her landlord had good taste in handymen. Kell was kind, competent and not too bad on the eyes either. She was so glad her first impression of him was wrong. She was also glad he didn't hold any ill will against her for smacking him with a plastic bat.

This could still be a scam, her inner thoughts warned. *Don't forget who he's working for.*

A dark cloud rained on her happy parade. Oh right, for a minute she'd been so excited about this place finally getting fixed she'd forgotten the possibility that Kell might be a spy for Donald. She'd been wrong about people before—just look at her jerk ex Larry.

Okay, so Kell might not be an angel. Maybe a devil in disguise? Whatever he was, she couldn't deny the fact that she needed him to fix up this place. If he was spying for Donald, all she had to do was make sure he didn't find anything to report back. She had to make sure he didn't find the secret room she was living in. That meant she needed to stay close to him while he was working here.

She glanced over at the way his forearm flexed as he wrote something on his clipboard, and her stomach did another somersault.

Sticking close to Kell wouldn't be a hardship. Remembering to keep her guard up would be.

"Any other basement issues?" Kell asked, marking something on his clipboard.

"There's a leak over in the far corner there."

She led him to the other side of the room where a small trickle of water was running down the wall onto the cement. The leak wasn't as bad as the one in her temporary bedroom, so she hadn't felt the need to address it yet. Now that Kell was here, she was going to mention every leak, flickering bulb and loose board in the theater. Hopefully he was being serious about being up for the challenge. Plus, the more work she gave him, the less he could be on the lookout for...other things.

Kell lifted his flashlight, pointing it up to the ceiling as he stared.

"Looks like the leak is coming from the floor above. Might even be above that. Do you have any other leaks anywhere?"

She huffed out a frustrated bark of laughter. "Only about a dozen."

Not counting the one in her secret bedroom.

Kell frowned. "Hmm, sounds like there may be roof issues if you have so many."

Exactly what she was thinking.

"A new roof is a big job, but if it's necessary I can call in my brothers."

"Brothers?" There were more of him? Were his brothers as helpful and as handsome as Kell? She shook her head. Not important. She'd promised herself after the humiliation of Larry leaving her high and dry, she'd be more practical when it came to love. She had to stop falling for every charming smile she saw. It only led to heartbreak.

Maybe what her best friend had always said was true: Maybe Piper's obsession with Disney movies as a child had warped her sense of what real relationships were supposed to be. But she wanted a love that inspired stories. One like her grandparents had. She swore she'd never seen two people more in love than Grandma and Grandpa. Sadly, chasing that dream had only led her to heartbreak. And what she needed to focus on right now was fixing up the theater, not scoring a date with a hottie handyman who might be a covert spy for her evil landlord. "Do they do contract work with you?"

He hesitated for a brief second before gracing her with a devastatingly charming smile. "Yeah. We have a company together. Most of the time we work separate contracts, but sometimes we work together on places."

"That's nice." She'd often wished for a sibling to play with, but sadly her parents divorced when she was ten and neither seemed interested in having any more kids. They'd barely been interested in her.

They moved on from the basement to the next floor where the dressing rooms and stage were. She took him through each of the five dressing rooms which, thankfully, needed nothing more than a few window frames repaired. The work needed in the backstage bathrooms would be a little more intensive. Three of the toilets didn't flush and nearly all the sinks dripped.

"Plumbing issues are common with old buildings like this," Kell said as he continued to make notes. "I don't think it'll need a full replumbing, but those sinks will need new faucets. I doubt Mr. Noll has ever replaced them."

She doubted her crummy landlord had ever replaced anything in this theater. Donald thought duct tape was an acceptable solution for any fix.

"How about the stage?" Kell asked, turning to her and motioning behind her.

She spun around, heart skipping a beat as she stared at her favorite place in the world. Making her way out of the bathroom, she moved backstage and sucked in a deep breath. Years of lingering smells sparked a plethora of happy memories. The powdery smell of stage makeup, dank musk of costumes worn over and over again, the sweet floral scent of roses from the bouquets brought to performers to celebrate and just a hint of tangy, stinky body odor. Those stage lights could make an ice cube sweat.

"The stage is perfect," she said as she stepped onto the floor. It was the one part of the theater she insisted Donald keep up to date and running perfectly. After all, what good was a theater without a proper stage?

Kell stepped onto the stage, glancing around. He nodded, seeming to agree with her assessment. As his eyes moved upward, he frowned. "What's that?"

She looked up to see what he was pointing at. Her red fabric was looped around a pulley, attached to the beams just below the stage lights.

"That? Oh, that's my sling. I'm preparing for a show next month."

He glanced over at her with a confused expression. "Sling? What kind of show uses a sling?"

She grinned. "An aerial show."

"Ariel? Like the mermaid?"

A giggle escaped her. She couldn't help it. The man was adorable when confused. "No, though we have done mermaid-themed shows. Aerials as in silks, lyra, sling, trapeze, rope and a ton of other apparatuses."

He continued to frown. Clearly not understanding her explanation. A thought popped into her head. Why tell him when she could show him?

"Stay right here," she said, rushing off the stage to the pulley system. Quickly she lowered her sling and secured the rope.

"Stand right there and don't move," she instructed as she came on stage and grasped the red fabric in her hands.

Standing with one leg in front of the other, she turned on her back foot before lifting into the air and mounting the sling with a front balance. She heard a small gasp from Kell, but she ignored it, continuing to shift her body in the fabric until she had the sling around her back. She spun in the air, speed increasing as she pulled her body into a straight line. Swooping out her legs, she did a flare, bringing herself into a straddle.

Once she was there, muscle memory took over as she crocheted each leg into the fabric. Using her core strength, she lifted her body up and grabbed the fabric, pulling her chest through as she continued to spin.

"Wow!"

Kell's soft exclamation made her smile. She loved seeing people experience aerials for the first time. Not that she could accurately see him as she was currently spinning too fast to see anything. But the awe in his voice gave her a picture. Wanting to give him just a little more of a wow factor, she decided to do a small drop. Engaging her core muscles, she dropped her hands, letting go of the fabric and falling forward. She heard a loud curse as Kell started to rush forward, but she'd safely landed in a T shape with her arms out, the sling securely around her back under her arms.

"I told you to stay put," she said with a small laugh as she lowered herself to the floor, sliding out of the sling.

"Yeah, but you didn't say you were going to go all daredevil stuntwoman and scare the life out of me. I thought you were going to crash into the stage and crack your skull open."

She chuckled. "Trust me, that's one of the easiest and safest drops there is."

He raised his eyebrows. "That's safe?"

"If you know how to do it properly, yes." She placed a hand on his arm. "But it was sweet of you to be worried."

Something in his eyes heated at her words. Her hand burned where she touched him. She quickly pulled her hand away, taking a small step back and glancing up at the sling. Good grief, the man was potent. She had to remember he was here to fix her theater, not date her.

"I've been doing aerials for thirteen years now. Started when I was fifteen and never broken a single bone. I promise it's safe if you do it properly."

That wasn't to say things couldn't go wrong. Even in the safest of environments with the proper training, accidents happened. While she'd never broken anything, she had had plenty of bruises, fabric burns and other small injuries over the years. Such was the life of a performer.

"It's like the Cirque du Soleil stuff then?"

She nodded. "Pretty much, but they tend to have more acts in their shows that we can't accommodate here."

No way would the Double Wheel of Destiny fit in this theater.

His gaze took in the theater, a curious expression on his face she couldn't decipher.

"Have you ever thought of finding a new place? One that could accommodate more…stuff. I'm sorry, I'm not sure what to call…" He waved a hand in the air at the hanging fabric.

She laughed softly. "We call them apparatuses, and no. I mostly focus on aerials, plus when I don't have an aerial show I rent the stage for stage plays and musicals. But I'm allowed to rent out the theater for performances," she rushed to say, in case he thought she was breaking her lease. Dang it! She'd forgotten the situation for a moment. She had to remember no matter how kind and handsome Kell was, she couldn't trust him.

He nodded, not giving any indication he was here as a spy for Donald. Until she knew for sure, she had to be careful. One slip and she could lose this place, her dream. She couldn't let that happen.

It had taken her years to get here. On her first day in aerial class as an anxious teenager who had only ever done community class gymnastics before, she'd known she'd found her calling. The very first spin in a hoop and she was hooked. She'd finally found a place she felt accepted, a place where she belonged. A place where her mind and body could be free to just exist without all the expectations of society. She knew, over her years of performing in traveling shows, that one day she wanted to provide that space for others. To teach aerials, put on her own shows, offer a welcoming place for those who needed it.

Which was why she had to make extra sure while giving Kell the tour that she skipped her secret bedroom. If Donald found *that* out, her butt would be kicked to the curb in a heartbeat.

"I've seen plenty of theater shows, but I've never been to an aerial show," he said, staring at the hanging fabric.

"Then I'll have to make sure you have a front-row seat at our next performance." Something inside her took flight at the thought of Kell sitting in the audience, watching her perform. Uh-oh, her romantic side was taking off again. Time to reel those thoughts in fast before she made a fool of herself again.

His bright blue gaze found hers, lighting up as his lips curved into a smile. "I'd love that. But maybe warn me how many death-defying drop things you're going to do so I don't overreact and rush up on stage to try and catch you."

A giggle escaped her lips. "You take the white knight thing seriously, don't you?"

He shrugged. "My brothers say I can be a bit overprotective."

Now that was something she wasn't used to. Her parents had taken a hands-off parenting style when she was a kid. She practically raised herself. She'd never had an overprotective partner. Most of the people she dated were other artists and performers. They knew she could handle herself and were generally too focused on their own stuff to worry about her. Except for Larry, but he wasn't overprotective. Larry was a loser who expected her to do all the housework, pay the bills and attend to his "needs" whenever he wanted. And then the jerk had the audacity to steal from her and run off.

Boy, could she pick 'em.

She wondered what it would be like to be with someone who worried about her well-being.

"Should we continue with the tour?" she asked.

He nodded. "Yes, we better continue. As...exciting as that demonstration was, I think we need to move on. If this place needs as much work as you say, it will take all day just to note everything down. I need to see every room in the place."

"You got it." She pasted on a smile, turning before he caught the lie in her eyes. She couldn't show him every room.

The storage room she'd turned into living quarters was at the end of a hall up a short staircase.

She'd turned the entry to her room into one of those secret bookcase doors and stashed stage props on the shelves in case anyone got curious. They could easily avoid that. She hoped. White knight or devious spy, she couldn't risk Kell finding out about her living arrangements. It was her little secret.

CHAPTER FOUR

KELL STOOD OUTSIDE of the Star-Crossed Theater, unable to keep the huge grin from widening his lips. A steady thrum of eager anticipation sped up his heart. Today was the first official workday for this project. He always got a rush of excitement when he got to do repairs. Something about working with his hands, fixing things, bringing life back to the broken, always made him feel… complete.

Selling a six-million-dollar property was a rush in itself, but the high died out quickly. Staring at a home or building he helped restore, seeing the light in people's eyes as they finally got a forever home—that's what stayed with him. Warming him in the dark, lonely nights, giving him a purpose.

But today felt like more than that.

He stared up at the towering building. He couldn't wait to work on all the much-needed repairs, but that wasn't the only reason for this buzzing feeling low in his gut.

Piper.

Her name whispered in his mind, filling his

chest with a warm sensation. The woman fascinated him. She was confident and beautiful and a bit odd. He couldn't put his finger on it, but there was something about her that drew him to her.

Bad idea, Kell.

He scowled as the thought popped into his head. A sigh left him, acknowledging the truth of it all. As intriguing as he found Piper, it would be a bad idea to do anything about it. For one, he didn't date. Kell was a casual-hookup-type guy. Relationships didn't work out for him. He'd learned long ago that love and happily-ever-afters were something other people got to have

Not him.

When a guy's ex found her soulmate immediately after breaking up with him—that was one thing. When it happened five times…that was a pattern. A pattern that told Kell he was destined to be nothing more than the stepping stone to other people's happy ending.

He refused to be stepped on any longer, which was why he'd sworn off dating. Couldn't get hurt if he didn't participate in the first place. Casual hookups were the safer bet.

He had no idea what type of dating Piper was into, but even if she was okay with his "no labels" policy, there was another reason he should not be entertaining romantic thoughts of her…

His phone rang, interrupting his musings. Pulling it from his pocket, he glanced at the screen with a scowl. And there it was. The reason he shouldn't pursue any type of hookup with Piper. Donald Noll's number flashed on his screen, reminding him of the second part of this job. The part Piper had no idea about. The part where he was basically betraying her by not telling her Donald was planning to sell the place right out from under her.

Swiping his thumb across the screen, he accepted the call and brought the phone to his ear.

"Mr. Noll," he said, affecting his cheery customer-service voice. "Did you receive my email?"

"What the hell, Thorson?"

That was a yes.

"There's at least twenty repairs on here that I did not stipulate," the angry voice hissed over the line.

Kell took a deep breath, counting to five. Over the years he'd dealt with his fair share of PITA clients, but Donald Noll took the cake. Every phone call, the guy was angry over something.

"Yes, Mr. Noll, but you did hire me to do a full inspection on the building. I'm simply reporting the issues I found during my inspection."

Donald snorted. "Right, and how much will these additional *issues* cost me in repairs? I know how you contractors work."

Kell's teeth ground together as he did his best not to lay into the jerk. He could remind Donald that he hired Kell to sell this building because he was getting a two-for-one deal in repairs, but somehow, he knew that would go right over the guy's head.

"I understand it's more work than we initially thought, but the better condition the building is in when we list it, the higher price we can get for it."

A humming sound came over the line. "I suppose that's true."

Kell knew bringing it back around to money would work. He could always spot the greedy ones a mile away. Good for his business, but lately he was beginning to wonder if it was damaging to his soul. More and more he found himself wishing he could spend more time working on Helping Homes and less on selling high-price properties. But the truth of the matter was if he and his brothers didn't continue their high-end real estate business, their charity would suffer. They sunk a lot of their profits into their charity, so sucking up to people like Donald Noll would have to continue.

"How many of these fixes do we have to do to bump the price up?"

A cold shudder of unease slicked its way down his spine. This was his least favorite part of the job. Flippers always hiked up the price to places whenever they did some cheap cosmetic fixes. Donald wasn't a flipper, but it was clear the guy just wanted to slap a new coat of paint on the building, add another million to the price and call it good.

Unfortunately for him, that wasn't going to work in this case.

"A lot of these fixes are necessary to even list the property," he replied, bracing himself for the reaction. He was answered by the expected string of angry curses.

"I thought you were the best real estate company in the Denver Metro area. What the hell are you talking about, Thorson? I hired you to make me money, not drive me into the poorhouse with repairs!"

Wow. Maybe Donald should audition for one of the plays the Star-Crossed hosted. The man was clearly dramatic enough.

"We can't list the property in the condition it's in," he replied in his most calming voice. "It won't pass inspection. You could list it 'as is' but that would drive the price down significantly. The type of buyers who will want this property don't want to put in a lot of repair work. They want a turnkey property."

He waited, listening to Donald grumble and mutter a few more choice curse words. After what felt like an eternity he spoke again.

"Fine, do what you have to do, but I want approval on any repair over a thousand."

He'd get approval on every repair no matter the cost. That was just smart business. He hadn't made it as far as he had in life by not getting things approved in writing.

"Of course. I'll start on the already-approved repairs and send you quotes before I start on the new issues I found."

"Good," Donald huffed. "Will any of this delay the listing?"

"It shouldn't. If anything big arises I can call my brothers in to help speed up the repairs. We should be able to put the listing on the market by the end of next month."

"Excellent. I want this place off my hands ASAP. As soon as that shrew's lease is up, I'm done with this albatross."

Kell clenched his jaw. It was bad business to tell your client to shove it where the sun doesn't shine, but the words were on the tip of his tongue. Piper was the furthest possible thing from a shrew. What kind of man called a woman a shrew anyway? A misogynist, that's what kind. Donald was that and more, but he was also Kell's client, so he held his tongue.

"Have you met her yet?" Donald asked.

"Ms. Pitts? Yes, I actually ran into her the other day when I came to do the inspection."

"Ha! Pitts. Perfect last name for that woman."

Kell's fist clenched as he held back his disgust at this man. His body vibrated with anger. What he wouldn't give to reach through the phone and punch the guy. But he couldn't. Good thing too, because that would probably void his contract and set him up for a lawsuit. Pity. Someone needed to teach Donald Noll some manners.

Needing to end this conversation before he did something stupid—like call his client a word his mother would ground him for, even as a fully grown adult—he rushed to speak.

"I'll send you an updated contract with the additional repairs to sign this evening. In the meantime, I'll get to work on the already-approved items."

Donald grunted out an agreement. But just as Kell was about to hang up, he spoke again.

"Thorson."

"Yes, Mr. Noll?"

"Remember to keep your lips zipped about the sale. I don't want Piper to catch wind of it and try and find a loophole to stay in the building. I wouldn't put it past a sneaky witch like her."

What was this guy's problem? Did his mother never hug him? From what Kell could tell, Piper was a sweet, caring person. Maybe Donald just had a stick up his butt because she expected him to actually do his job as a landlord and fix all the broken crap around the place. How awful that must be for him.

Regulating his voice the best he could, he gripped the phone tighter as he replied. "I really think it would be better if you informed your tenant you won't be renewing her lease. That way she can start looking for a new theater."

"I don't really give a rat's turd what you think, Thorson. You work for me, so keep your lips zipped or our contract is in breach, and I'll sue you for everything you're worth."

Which in addition to his vast wealth would also be his charity. Dammit! How had he gotten himself stuck between a rock and this jerkwad? Sucking in a deep, calming breath, he spoke between clenched teeth.

"Yes, Mr. Noll. I understand. I won't say a word."

"Good. Now get to work."

He could remind the guy that even though he was contracted to work for him, Donald was not his boss, but the line went dead as the jerk hung up. Slipping his phone back into his pocket he closed his eyes, counting to ten as he focused on his breathing. When he opened his eyes back up, he felt most of the rage melt away. It was still there, simmering in his gut. He feared it would remain until this hellscape of a job was over.

He made his way inside the building, heading past the front into the theater where he spied a sight that made his anger ease, and the warmth return to his chest. There she was. The reason not everything about this job was hell.

Piper stood on the stage adjusting a long dark purple sling. He knew what they were called now, thanks to her. There were six others set up on stage in various colors. They hung about six inches off the ground. Much lower than the one she had up the other day when she nearly gave him a heart attack with that drop thing she did.

He stood there and watched her for a moment. The joy on her face as she touched the fabric of the sling, flipping it so it lay perfectly for her students. Her care and attention to detail showed how much she loved her job, loved this theater. Rage started to rise in him again at Donald. How could the man think such awful things about Piper?

Not wanting to scare her again, he announced himself as he approached the stage.

"Hey there."

She glanced over at him, a warm smile lighting up her face. His breath caught in his chest at her beauty. What the hell was wrong with him? He barely knew her, and yet his heart was pounding in his chest from a simple smile. This was not good. He refused to fall down this rabbit hole again. No feelings. Just fun. That was his motto and he was sticking to it, no matter who life tossed in his path.

"Kell, it's so good to see you." Her cheeks flushed as the words left her lips. "I mean, it's good that you're here. Because you're fixing stuff, and we need stuff fixed and so that's why you're here and that's why it's good…yeah."

She turned, suddenly very interested in fussing with the sling in front of her. He dipped his head to hide a smile at her flustered attitude. This spark between them might be a bad idea, but damn if he didn't enjoy it just a little.

His happiness dimmed as he remembered what he was really doing here. The secret he was keeping from her. Bet she wouldn't smile so kindly at him if she knew he was about to sell this place out from under her. Guilt churned in his gut.

Dammit. He was no better than Donald.

CHAPTER FIVE

COULD SHE EVER be in the presence of this man and not embarrass herself?

Piper fussed with the perfectly hung sling, avoiding eye contact after her awkward overexplanation. Thankfully, Kell was a gentleman and didn't call attention to her rambling.

"Are you starting the repairs today?" she asked, still focused on the red fabric hanging in front of her.

"If that works for you."

His warm, deep voice sent a shiver of desire down her spine. She told her body to knock it off. She had a class in fifteen minutes. Her brain needed to be focused on instruction, not mooning over a hot guy. Maybe she just needed to hop back into the dating pool. It had been four months since Larry the Loser took off in the middle of the night with all her savings, leaving her with no way to pay the rent on their apartment. Which was why she'd been secretly crashing at the theater ever since.

Damn you, Larry!

A sigh escaped her. Larry's leaving hadn't hurt as much as his betrayal. If she was honest with herself, she might have jumped the gun on moving in with him. They'd only been dating a few months, and she let her romantic notions carry her away. Truth be told, after Larry left, she nursed a broken heart for three weeks. Shorter than her previous heartbreaks, but no less painful. Then one day she realized the stealing hurt more than the leaving. She'd simply let herself get swept up in the romance of a new relationship…again. She had to stop doing that.

"Works for me," she replied, finally turning to face him, pushing thoughts of jerk exes and money problems out of her mind. "I have a couple of classes today, but we're going to be on the stage so as long as we don't get in your way, it should be fine."

His brow furrowed, head tilting as he stared at her with a contemplative expression.

"As long as you don't get in my way? I think you've got that backward. I'm here to do repairs around your schedule. I'm the one that should worry about getting in the way."

She laughed off the comment. That might be the case, but years of masking and people-pleasing was a hard habit to break.

As a kid, she had found it easier to put everyone else's needs ahead of her own. She learned early on if she made a fuss, all that happened was punishment. Her parents hadn't been physically abusive, they never hit her or anything. But they also found her difficult and told her so on numerous occasions. They hated that she couldn't eat certain foods, were annoyed when she said clothes felt too tight or scratchy, got embarrassed when she cried at loud noises or bright lights.

When she finally got her autism diagnosis, she'd been fifteen and shuffling between her parents' houses. By then they'd basically washed their hands of her. The calls on birthdays and Christmas were their only communication these days, and that worked out fine for her. Still, it was hard for her not to bend over backward to make sure everyone around her was comfortable. Even if it meant she was on edge.

Kell walked up to the end of the stage, setting his tool bag down on the floor. He placed his elbows on the stage floor and leaned against the edge, staring up at her with a pleasant but serious expression.

"Where can I work today that won't be in your way?"

He was asking her? She wasn't used to that. Usually the people Donald hired—the few he had over the years—were rude and pushy. They didn't care that she had a business to run. Kell was different. Too different. Her instincts screamed. Maybe Donald hired Mr. White Knight here to throw her off her game. The possibility he was in league with her enemy was high. Too high for her to go all googly eyes over a few kind gestures and a sinfully sexy smile. She needed to keep her cards close to her chest.

And by cards, she meant her secret living arrangements. Time to throw him off the scent and away from her hidden bedroom.

"Um…" She filtered through the list of repairs he'd mentioned the other day on their tour, trying to sift through them all to make a decision. Pressure had her nerves rising. She wasn't used to being the one calling the shots. In her aerial studio, sure, but not in building repairs.

"Sorry." Kell held up a hand. "Let me make this easier on you. I was planning on working down in the basement on the electrical today. I will have to turn off the power for a while, which means no lights for a few hours. Is that okay?"

Relief filled her as he presented her with a clear plan. The yes-or-no answer was much simpler for her frazzled brain to process. And the basement was about as far away from her room as possible.

"Yes, that would be fine." She smiled, opening the sling and sinking down into it. The fabric swayed as she sat facing him, her feet rocking her back and forth along the stage floor. The soothing motion calmed her nerves. "With the windows, we'll get plenty of summer sun for light, so no overhead lights shouldn't be a problem."

He nodded with a smile. "Sounds like a plan then. How many classes do you have today?"

"Four," she said, pausing for a moment. A frown turned down her lips as a thought occurred to her. "But we do have rehearsal tonight at seven. The sun sets around nine, but the light will be much dimmer. We might need the overheads for the evening rehearsal."

"Not a problem." Kell reached down to grab his clipboard out of his tool bag. He scanned the paper on it before looking back up at her with a confident smile. "I should be done before five."

Right, because he had a job with normal hours. Nothing was normal when you were in the arts. Piper supposed he might have contractor emergencies that called him out at odd hours. Unless he didn't offer that service. Honestly, she had no idea. She didn't even know what his business was called. Wasn't like she was the one who hired him after all. He could be a guy Donald found at the grocery store that had a hammer and worked for cheap. Sounded like something her landlord would do.

A tiny voice in the back of her hear told her to search him out on the web, but she ignored it. Wasn't like she was going to date the guy. No need to vet him. Besides, she'd seen the invoice with Donald's signature. His work here was legit, no matter where Donald had found him.

And even if he was spying for Donald, Kell didn't seem like the shady contractor type of guy.

She'd bet he had all the licensing and permits he needed…she hoped. As long as he made this place safe and whole again, she didn't care. Let Donald worry about the legality of everything. She was just happy things were finally getting fixed around here.

"I have two classes this morning and then two after lunch. The last one ends at four in the afternoon so we should still be good with no lights as far as all the classes go."

He inclined his head. "Then I'll make sure you have overheads before I leave."

She smiled, continuing to sway in the sling. "There's that white knight attitude again."

With a small chuckle, he gave her a dramatic bow, placing his hand over his heart. "My lady."

She giggled. The man was utterly charming.

"What classes do you have today?"

She looked out into the audience as she went over her classes in her mind. "This afternoon I have advanced lyra and rope."

"Lyra?" he asked, his face scrunching up in confusion.

"Hoop," she replied.

"Like a Hula-Hoop?"

A snort of laughter escaped her. "Um, no. If you rigged a Hula-Hoop, it would break the second you tried to mount it. Lyras, or hoops, are steel. A plastic Hula-Hoop could never support a person's weight."

"Steel?" His dark eyebrows rose as a soft whistle left his lips. "Sounds heavy."

She nodded. "They can be, especially if you have a solid one. The hollow ones are much lighter, but the solid ones maintain your spin better."

"Interesting," he said, gaze focused on her, eyes bright with curiosity. "Is the fabric a special material too?"

She grinned, his genuine interest prompting her to info dump in excitement.

"Yes. Aerial silks are generally made from nylon tricot, polyester tricot or polyester Lycra. Each fabric gives a slightly different stretch depending on what you need. But they're all highly durable and, when rigged correctly, can hold five thousand pounds."

His eyes widened. "Five thousand pounds?"

"Yup." She nodded. "You have to make sure you account for the drop force in aerials. A good aerial studio will make sure they can rig the weight of a car. I always tell people who are worried about weight that aerials is for every body type. Apparatuses can be adjusted for any ability. Aerials is for everyone."

She gave him a pointed look. He laughed, waving a hand in the air.

"Oh no. I saw that drop thing you did yesterday. You say aerials is for everyone, but I say I'm much happier with my feet on the ground."

"I'll get you up here one of these days," she teased.

He shook his head. "I guess you're doing the fabric classes this morning?"

He motioned to the sling she was sitting in. She nodded.

"Yes, I have a sensory sling class and then youth beginner sling after that."

"Sensory sling? What's that?"

She sucked in a sharp breath. He'd made her feel so comfortable, so at ease, she'd forgotten he was basically a stranger to her. She took a deep breath, preparing to explain and hoping he was the type of person who wouldn't be a judgmental jerk. She didn't think he would but…you never knew.

"It's a class for children with sensory needs. Kids who have autism, Sensory Processing Disorder, ADHD. The spinning and wrapping of aerial sling can help regulate their nervous system."

She watched his face as she explained, looking for signs of judgment. When she saw nothing but contemplation, she pressed on, revealing something she rarely did with people she didn't know well.

"It's actually how I found aerials." She paused, watching his face carefully. "My doctor suggested it after I got my autism diagnosis as a way to regulate and find a community of friends."

And, boy, had the doctor been right. Aerials had saved her during a time she felt her lowest.

Kell's thoughtful expression morphed into a warm smile. "Huh, wonder if I could get my brother Mal up in one of these things. He's on the spectrum too. Though he's not too big into community. More of a loner. Keeps to himself a lot."

She could understand that. There were plenty of times she got overstimulated and just wanted to be alone.

"But now I'm afraid you have more ammo to try and get me up into one of these things," Kell continued. "Though I can't see how spinning around and trying not to break my neck in a fall would help my ADHD."

He gave her a wink that made her heart practically beat out of her chest. Not only was he not judgmental about her neurodiversity, but he was also neurodivergent! No wonder they seemed to click so well.

Don't trust him, Piper! He's the enemy!

She scoffed at her inner voice. *Enemy* was a bit of a stretch, but her subconscious was right to remind her she didn't know this man well. Or what his true intentions might be. Tucking away that knowledge, she grinned.

"Mark my words, Kell," she said, pointing a finger at him. "Before you finish the repairs on this place, I will get you up into an apparatus."

He chuckled, waving off her promise. "Would you look at the time. I better get off to work. Lots of things to fix, wires and leaks and such."

He bent down and grabbed his bag, moving past the stage to the hallway leading down to the basement.

"You'd be surprised how fun it is," she called after him.

"Can't hear you," he playfully yelled back. "Too busy thinking about how my feet are safely on the ground."

She laughed as he disappeared. Relief filled her entire body. Normally she didn't tell people about her autism until she'd known them for a while. It wasn't that she was ashamed of being autistic. There was nothing wrong with being on the spectrum. But not everyone felt that way. She'd had dates break things off after finding out. Friends pull away. People treated her like she had some horrible disease instead of simply a difference in neurological pathways.

Happiness filled her as Kell not only accepted her reveal, but understood.

Loud shouts of tiny voices filled the air as the kids for her sensory class started to rush into the theater. She put thoughts of sweet, sexy handymen away, focusing on the class about to start. But maybe she'd check in with Kell after her morning classes. She had to make sure he wasn't seeing anything he wasn't supposed to. And if it happened to be lunchtime, maybe they could grab a bite together. After all, they both had to eat, didn't they?

CHAPTER SIX

TWO AND A half hours later, Piper waved goodbye to the students of her youth sling group. The morning classes had gone by without a hitch today. Thank goodness. Kids' classes tended to be a bit harried. Listening was a skill not all of them had perfected yet, which was to be expected. You had to have real patience to teach kids, and it took a special skill to teach the neurodivergent kiddos. Thankfully she knew what they needed because it was often the same thing she needed.

Understanding, patience, clear instructions and caring.

She just wished more people understood that.

The lights above the stage flickered for a moment before turning on full brightness. She squinted, averting her eyes as the stage filled with harsh artificial light.

"Guess that means he fixed them," she said, daisy-chaining the sling she'd just taken down. "One problem down."

A hundred more to go.

She gathered all the chained slings and placed

them in their cubbies just off the stage. There were a few hours until her afternoon classes. Enough time to run out and grab lunch. She should check if Kell wanted lunch…and check in on him in general. There wasn't any evidence of her squatting in the basement, but she needed to be vigilant anytime the man was here. If that meant she had to spend more time in the presence of the sweet and sexy man, so be it.

With butterflies taking flight in her stomach, she made her way down to the basement, hoping to find him still there. She did. He was crouched at the far end of the basement near the fuse box, placing tools and wires inside his bag.

"Got the lights fixed, I see," she said, chuckling softly at her own joke.

He glanced up at her, a smile curling his full lips. Holy cow! The man was unfairly handsome when he smiled. Her mind was going to all the naughty places it had no business going.

"Yup." He stood, brushing his hands off on his dark jeans. "Replaced some fuses, fixed some of the faulty wiring. You should be good to go now. As far as light anyhow."

Like she said, one of a hundred.

"That's good news, considering we have a show coming up and it'd be awfully hard to perform in the dark."

"What's the show?"

"It's an aerial performance of the most romantic story ever written, *Romeo and Juliet*."

He frowned. "*Romeo and Juliet* isn't a romance. Don't seven people die in that play?"

She waved away his denial. "Six actually, but that's not the point. It's a story of passion and how far a person is willing to go for true love."

"It's a cautionary tale about teenage hormones and impulsiveness."

Okay, then. It seemed like someone was a true-love doubter.

Kell uncuffed his flannel shirt, then rolled the sleeves up his arms before crossing them over his chest. She did not notice how muscled his fore-arms were. Not one bit. Her mind was still focused on how this man who was usually so positive and cheerful could hate a timeless classic like *Romeo and Juliet*.

"It's called *The Tragedy of Romeo and Juliet* for a reason," he pointed out.

She scowled at him. "Don't tell me you're one of those people."

Dark eyebrows rose on his forehead. "What people?"

"The kind who hate love and happily-ever-afters."

He frowned, letting out a contemplative sigh. "I don't hate love. I just don't think it exists for everyone. And *Romeo and Juliet* did not end in a happily-ever-after. Therefore, not a romance."

A slight sting of irritation wriggled in her gut.

"Let me guess," he said with a knowing grin. "You're a stars-in-the-eyes hopeless romantic who believes everyone has a perfect soulmate out there just waiting for them."

She sniffed, taking umbrage with his accurate assessment of her. "Maybe. Is that such a bad thing?"

He shook his head, his smile turning soft. "No. I think it's great actually. But unfortunately, that's not the way the world works. Not everyone gets their happily-ever-after. In fact, some people are stepping stones for everyone else's happy ending."

What did he mean by that?

Before she could ask, he continued.

"But *Romeo and Juliet* still isn't a romantic story. It's one of Shakespeare's tragedies. 'For never was a story of more woe than this of Juliet and her Romeo.'"

"Fixes lights and memorizes Shakespeare." She arched one eyebrow at him. "The man has layers."

He chuckled, shaking his head. "Not really. My mother was on the board for the Denver Performing Arts Center for years. We went to all the shows as kids. Saw a lot of Shakespeare. Guess it kind of stuck."

A board member of an arts community? Who were his parents? Didn't seem like the kind of position the parent of a contractor would have.

Once again, she was reminded how little she knew about Kell.

"You don't believe in love?" she asked. "Like, at all?"

He leaned back against the hard brick wall. His brow furrowed as he stared past her, not focusing on anything in particular. If she had to guess, she would say he wasn't staring at anything in the room at all. He looked the way she felt when she was going over memories in her mind. Pensive and…sad.

"I believe in the love you have for your family, your friends, pets—if you have them—and I do think some people out there find a forever kind of love." He paused, furrow turning into a hopeless frown. "But I know that kind of stuff isn't for me. True love…isn't my style."

"That's a pretty pessimistic way to think." She slapped a hand over her mouth, knowing blurting that out had been rude. She hadn't meant to. It just slipped out. Sometimes her mouth was faster than her brain and she said the wrong thing.

Kell stared at her for a moment then burst out laughing. Her face flamed, not sure why her comment was so funny or if he was laughing at her. She didn't think it was the latter. Kell might not believe in love like she did, but the man wasn't cruel.

"I think that's the first time someone has called me pessimistic," he said, his laughter dying down.

"Normally that's my brother Mal's nickname. He's gonna get a chuckle out of this when I tell him."

Grateful he was laughing at the scenario and not her, she pressed on. "Not a single one of your significant others called you pessimistic when learning about your 'no true love' belief?"

She would have called him out for sure.

He winced. "Eh, I'm not really into labels. I'm more of a 'let's have fun until we're done' type guy."

The way he said that felt like something more. She heard an undertone of pain in his carefree words.

"Not into labels. Very original," she teased. "No guy in the history of the universe has ever said that to cover for his commitment phobia."

He took a step forward and bopped her on the nose with his finger. "And a true romantic who believes in happily-ever-after—not cliché for an art lover at all."

She ducked her head to hide the flush she felt rising on her cheeks at his touch.

Down, body. He doesn't believe in love. He might turn me in to Donald. He's not for us. No matter how sexy and sweet we find him. Stop falling so fast—remember what happened with Larry. Don't play the fool again.

"Might be cliché, but it does sell tickets. Which is why we are billing our *Romeo and Juliet* aerial show with the tagline *Romance in the Skies*."

He nodded. "Sounds like I better get my ticket before they sell out."

She snorted out a strangled laugh. "No worries there. We've barely sold any tickets, and the show is in less than four weeks. We'll be lucky if we get half a house."

A heavy sigh left her. It was always a struggle to pack the theater for a show, but lately it seemed like no one wanted to venture out to see live theater. She could really use a sold-out show.

"Low ticket sales?" His lips turned down, brow wrinkling. "But it sounds so cool. I would think everyone would want to see an aerial performance."

She shrugged, thinking the same thing, but the truth was in the lack of ticket sales. "People love consuming art, but they don't like supporting it with their money. I don't know, maybe I'll run a half-off ticket sale closer to the show date."

She'd lose money, but at least there'd be people in the audience to cheer for her students. They deserved it.

"Hmm." Kell brought a hand up to stroke his chin. "Don't discount tickets just yet. I may have some ideas to pack the house."

"You have ideas to sell tickets to an aerial show?"

Dropping his hand, he grinned at her. "My mom was on an arts board, remember? Plus, my family has…experience in getting people to support certain causes."

Okay, that didn't sound cryptic and suspicious at all. Suspicious or not, she was grateful. She needed all the help she could get. The way her finances were, she wasn't above selling her soul to fill the house.

A loud grumbling sound filled the room. Her face flamed as she realized the sound came from her stomach. Kell, bless his heart, pretended not to hear a thing. It did remind her of the initial reason she came down here. To ask him to lunch. And check to make sure he wasn't spying for Donald, but he didn't need to know that last part.

"Are you taking a lunch break or moving on to the next task?" She didn't want to interrupt his work if he was in a flow. She hated when people did that to her.

He reached down to his bag and pulled out his clipboard, looking over the papers on it.

"I could break for lunch. I was planning on starting in on the bathrooms after fixing the lights. Figured that was the next highest priority."

Yes please, especially with the show coming up. Those back bathrooms would be in full use by the cast. Having them up and running with no leaks or plugs would be wonderful.

"I was just heading out to grab a bite if you want to tag along," she said. There. That sounded like something a friend would say.

He leaned down to tuck the clipboard back into his bag, smiling as he rose again. "Sounds great. What do you have in mind?"

So many things when it came to this man. Things she should absolutely not have in mind considering the odds of them ever happening. Zero. Swallowing down what she really wanted to say, she smiled and asked, "How do you feel about tacos?"

CHAPTER SEVEN

KELL LOVED TACOS. They were the perfect food in his opinion. Spicy meat and delicious veggies all wrapped up in a corn tortilla you could pop into your mouth. He would never say no to getting tacos. Which is how he found himself leaving the theater with Piper to grab a friendly lunch.

He said *friendly* because he noticed a very clear shift in her attitude toward him when he said he didn't believe in true love. Her body had gone rigid, the flirty spark in her eyes snuffed out. He'd ruined any chance of them exploring their chemistry the moment he doom-and-gloomed all over her fairy-tale beliefs.

Which was for the best, considering he was betraying her trust by keeping the sale a secret. The stinging burn of guilt and anger scorched his chest. Damn Donald to eternity.

On the one hand he regretted his decision. He felt a magnetic pull toward this woman. One he desperately wanted to explore. But on the other hand, he believed in being honest when it came to relationships. Point one, the fact that he didn't do them. It would be cruel to lead Piper on, knowing he could never give her the commitment she desired.

Which led him here, walking by her side on a sunny summer day toward Civic Park where a line of food trucks sat. Delicious smells filled the air the closer they got. Each one held the unique scent of their trade-food style. His stomach growled, wishing it was bigger so he could sample each and every delicacy. He'd have to make a point to come here for lunch every day he worked this job so he could try all the options offered.

"Are these trucks here every day?" he asked, pointing to the row of vehicles.

"Yup." Piper smiled at him. "Every day, rain or shine. Except in the winter, I guess. Once the snow starts, the season kind of shuts down for a lot of them."

Made sense. He wondered what the business owners did in the winter months. Selling property was a year-round gig. Though the spring through fall seasons were the most profitable, he and his brothers still made deals during the winter months.

"Wait until you try these tacos." Piper clasped her hands together, rubbing them as her gaze filled with hungry anticipation. "They're the best in the world!"

He seriously doubted that. He'd been all over the world. Sampled cuisine from top chefs and family-run restaurants that had been in operation for generations. No way could a small taco truck in Colorado be the best in the world.

"That's an awfully high bar you set there," he said, glancing over at her as they took their spot in the back of the very long line for the taco truck.

"It's true." She nodded. "In fact, let's bet on it."

"Bet?"

"If you agree that these are the best tacos you've ever eaten, which they will be, you have to let me give you an aerial lesson."

He blinked, a ball of anxiety crawling up his throat at her words. "Excuse me?"

She laughed. "You heard me. If you agree these are the best tacos in the world then you have to get up in the apparatus of my choice and I'll teach you some aerial moves."

Why in the world would he ever need to learn aerial moves? They were cool and fun to look at, but the thought of doing that spinny drop thing she did the other day horrified him.

"Come on, Kell," she said, when he continued to stare at her, not speaking. "You can't tell me you're scared of being a few feet off the ground on a stage. You work on roofs, right? That's way higher than a sling."

He shook his head, taking a small step forward with her as the line moved. "It's not the height, it's the falling and breaking my neck."

"People fall off roofs all the time and break stuff."

He frowned, having had a few close calls with that himself over the years. Very unpleasant memories. "Thank you for that reminder, but I'm not actively throwing myself to the ground when I'm working. You, however, with the spinning and dropping, seem to be tempting fate every day."

She lifted one shoulder in a small shrug. "It's fun."

He snorted. "You have an odd definition of fun."

A heavy sigh left her. "So I've been told."

Shoot! He hadn't meant it like that. He'd just been teasing her, but he could see how his words could come across as insensitive. His brother Mal misinterpreted his intentions when he wasn't clear enough at times too.

"I'm sorry, I didn't mean—"

Piper waved a hand in the air, a soft smile tilting her lips. "It's okay, I understood what you meant. But there are some people who think what I do is…silly."

What? Who? He thought her aerial stuff was amazing. Stunning and beautiful. A dance form and an athletic achievement. Not necessarily something he wanted to try for himself, but he enjoyed watching her do it. When he wasn't terrified she'd fall and break her neck that is.

"My parents never understood my love of aerials, and those who aren't in the community tend to get annoyed when I go on a tangent talking about all the different apparatuses, or the history of aerial arts. I know it can be boring for people who aren't into it. I just love it so much."

He shook his head. "Boring is the last thing I'd call it, and anyone who dismisses your passion is the one who's boring. Special interests are great. One time in high school I saw a video about deck building. Something in me clicked and I spent the next month hyperfocused on learning every step of the deck-building process from ground prep, to post holing, to framing and sealant."

She grinned up at him, a teasing light entering those dark brown eyes. "Does that mean you accept the bet?"

Didn't seem like she was going to let this go. He chuckled softly, admiring her determination to get him to try aerials. Yeah, not going to happen. But since he had extreme confidence that while this truck's tacos smelled amazing, they certainly weren't going to be the best he'd ever had, there was no risk in saying yes. But…

"What do I get if I win?" He tilted his head and stared down at her, way down because the petite woman was at least a foot shorter than his six-one.

Her face scrunched up as he posed the question. "It doesn't matter because I'm going to win."

"So confident," he laughed softly. "But that's not a very fair bet. There have to be stakes. You could lose."

She waved a hand in the air as if the very idea

was preposterous. "Not going to happen, but I suppose you are right. The bet needs to be even."

The line moved ahead again. Piper scooted forward, leaving a larger-than-usual amount of space between her and the customer in front of her. The guy behind him was so close he could smell the dude's breath. It wasn't pleasant. But it didn't bother him too much to be packed tightly in line. Piper seemed to be bothered by it very much, judging from the way she intentionally left space and the way her fingers kept tapping against her thighs. He wished the line would move faster so they could grab their food and move somewhere with less people.

An idea popped into his head. The words were out of his mouth before he thought about it. "I can grab the tacos if you want to find a place for us to sit and eat."

Piper's thoughtful expression fell into one of confusion. "What?"

Clearing his throat, he lowered his voice and leaned down so the people around them wouldn't hear. "You seem…uncomfortable. I don't mean to assume, but my brother Mal hates crowds too. Gets kind of tense and fidgety in them."

His gaze moved down to her fingers, which stopped tapping immediately and closed into a fist. Damn, he'd made it worse. Now he'd implied she should hide herself. Not his intentions at all.

"I didn't mean to upset you," he said. "I simply

wanted to give you an option if waiting in line was overwhelming you."

A million emotions passed over her face. They flew by in a rush, too fast for him to identify them. Finally, she graced him with a soft, somewhat sad smile.

"It's too bad you don't believe in love because you'd make great boyfriend material."

He snorted out a laugh. Yeah, that was that problem. He'd been a great boyfriend before, but each time, no matter how caring and attentive he'd been, every relationship had been missing that spark. Considering each of his exes found the spark with their very next partner, Kell had come to the conclusion he was the flint to start the fire…

For everyone else but him.

Terrible but true.

"Thank you for the offer," Piper continued. "But I'm okay. Do I hate crowds? Yes, but the tacos are worth it. And don't think you're getting out of the bet by being sweet, mister." She pointed a finger at him, the teasing light entering her eyes again.

Grateful that he hadn't offended her, he teased back. "Technically I haven't agreed to the bet yet. You're still avoiding the stakes if I win."

"Never gonna happen, but okay. What do you want if you win?"

A date with you.

No. He couldn't say that. Piper had made her stance on dating versus hookups very clear. As much as he'd love to take her on a date that ended with making her breakfast at his place the following morning, he knew it would only end badly. Considering he'd be seeing her every day for the next six weeks, a situation like that could get uncomfortable fast. Plus, there was the pesky little detail of the huge secret he was keeping from her.

The second she found out he not only knew about the theater sale but was the realtor in charge of selling it…she'd hate him for sure.

His gut cramped. Bitter anger and resentment at Donald rose again. Damn the man for being a coward and not telling his tenant he was selling. And damn himself for signing that stupid contract with the NDA.

Nothing to do about it now but move forward.

"Hmm, let's see." He stroked his chin, thinking about something appropriate he could use as betting stakes. "Oh, I know. If I win you have to let me help you fill the seats for your show."

She blinked. "I don't think you know how betting works. It sounds like I win in both outcomes."

True. But he couldn't tell her he was feeling guilty. This was penance for his upcoming offence. Perhaps if he helped her sell out the show, she'd have enough funds to find a new theater and wouldn't hate him. He had no idea why he cared so much if this woman he barely knew hated him or not, but he did.

He shrugged, not wanting to reveal anything. "If you don't want to bet then—"

"Nope," she quickly interrupted. "Bet's on, sucker."

She stuck out her hand. He grinned, grasping it with his own. His large hand engulfed hers as they shook. He could feel the coarse calluses on her palm, no doubt from her aerial training. Despite the roughness, her hand was warm and delicate. The feel of her skin against his heated his entire being. A bolt of desire shot straight down to his core. Damn. Why did he have to be attracted to the one woman he couldn't have?

She sucked in a harsh breath, her eyes filling with need as her hand pressed against his. He pulled her closer, his body refusing to listen to his brain. Thinking only of the woman it wanted in front of him. Piper went willingly. Stepping closer to him until their bodies were a hairbreadth apart. Her lips parted, catching his attention with their plump, pink temptation. His head started to lean down of its own accord. Her eyes went hazy, lids dropping as she rose on her toes and—

"Next in line!"

The shout broke the spell.

Piper's eyes opened wide as her cheeks flushed a pretty pink. She dropped his hand and stepped forward toward the order window, avoiding eye contact. Damn, that was a close one. They'd almost forgotten they were all wrong for each other.

"A number three, please and—" She paused, turning to him. "What do you want?"

You.

"Dealers choice," he said to her, unable to think of anything but the huge mistake they almost made.

She nodded, turning back to the man in the truck. "Two number threes, please."

He reached for his wallet, but Piper paid before he could get it out.

"I got it." She waved him away when he tried to give her cash. "I invited you so it's my treat. Unless you hate the tacos. Then that's blasphemy and you can pay me back."

He chuckled, grateful the awkwardness had passed, and she was back to teasing again.

Their order was up in record time. He grabbed the two paper containers each holding three delicious-looking corn tortillas filled with ground meat, chopped onions and peppers, slices of avocado and some green on top that looked like cilantro. He brought one container to his face and sniffed.

"Yup, cilantro," he confirmed.

"Oh, shoot!" Piper stared at him in horror as he placed the dishes down on the picnic table she'd picked out for them to enjoy their lunch. "I forgot to ask if you're a cilantro-tastes-like-soap person before ordering."

"Worried you'll lose the bet?" He grinned, taking a seat on the bench.

She sat across from him, grabbing her food and pulling it to her. "Ha! Not a chance. Even cilantro haters love these tacos. But I might suggest you pick it off if you hate it."

He grabbed one of the tacos in his hand and shook his head. "No soapy taste for me. I love cilantro."

"Oh good, me too." Lifting her own taco, she raised it high in the air. "To getting you up in a hoop, or sling, or maybe loops."

He wasn't sure what that last one was, but unfortunately for her he wasn't getting up in any of them because she wasn't going to win. Still, he raised his own taco.

"To me filling your theater on opening night."

She rolled her eyes, bringing the taco to her lips and biting down. A soft, pleasure filled moan left her lips as she took her first bite. He shifted on the bench, reminding himself she was enjoying the food and his body needed to chill. To distract himself he took his own bite.

One second in, he knew he was screwed.

Flavors exploded on his tongue. Rich, meaty, spicy, pure heaven wrapped in a corn tortilla. His eyes closed as a deep moan came from his own throat. Piper had been right. These were the best damn tacos he'd ever had in his life.

Oh no.

He opened his eyes to find her staring at him with triumphant glee all over her face.

"Come on," she prodded. "Say it."

Not wanting to admit defeat yet, he shoved the rest of the taco in his mouth, enjoying the delectable taste of his doom before responding. "Fine. You're right. These are the best tacos I've ever had."

"Yes! I told you. Ooh, I can't wait to get you in the air."

He wondered how long he could hold this off. Something told him the experience was going to be extremely embarrassing. Hoping to distract her from making any solid plans, he came up with an idea.

"I'm still helping you fill seats for the show."

She paused with her taco halfway to her mouth. "You really don't know how betting works, do you? Suit yourself. Honestly, I can use all the help I can get, and you need to get more familiar with aerials anyway."

He ignored the excited little squeak as she added that last bit and focused instead on how he could help her sell out her show to absolve his betrayal.

CHAPTER EIGHT

"Who is the hottie handyman?"

Piper glanced over at the question. Rachel, her best friend and ex-girlfriend, sat on the stage, stretching out her straddle. Rachel's dark green eyes were curious as they stared up into the audience where Kell was fixing some of the broken carpet grippers on the stairs. Not top priority fixes, but Piper had tripped and nearly tumbled down them yesterday. Kell had seen and moved the repair up his list immediately, claiming it needed to be fixed before the show so no one in the audience hurt themselves.

She hadn't argued with that. The last thing she needed on top of all her money troubles was an injury lawsuit.

"Shh!" She scowled at Rachel. "Not so loud! He'll hear you."

"And he is…"

"Kellen. Donald hired him to fix up stuff around here."

Rachel let out a relieved sigh, pointing and flexing her toes as she continued to stretch. "Finally!

I swear I didn't think that jerk was ever going to fix anything around here."

"Same," Piper agreed, moving her legs together and bringing her nose to her knees. Her voice came out slightly muffled as she continued to explain Kell's presence. "But I guess all my emails finally got through. He showed up the other day and has been hard at work ever since."

With each passing day her suspicions that Kell was a spy started to slip away. She was still being vigilant, but a small flicker of trust started to grow. Flaming brighter with every sweet deed he completed.

"Sounds like Donald finally hired a competent contractor."

"And he's sweet too, considering how we met." Oops! She hadn't meant to say that out loud. Too late. Rachel's head whipped her way, eyes wide.

"How did you meet?"

A soft groan left her. She glanced around the stage where the cast was warming up for the afternoon's rehearsal. Knowing her best friend wasn't going to let this go, she lowered her voice and spoke.

"I kind of thought he was a robber and hit him with a Wiffle Ball bat."

"What?"

"Shh!"

A few curious eyes, including Kell's, glanced

their way. Piper ducked her head, deepening her stretch and hiding her embarrassment.

"You have to tell me everything," Rachel said gleefully. "Right now."

With a heavy sigh, she launched into the explanation of the morning she'd heard noises on the stage and thought Kell was there to steal things… or worse.

"He was very sweet about it when I explained," she said after getting the whole story out. "He even apologized for scaring me and asked me to show him every fix needed, including the ones Donald didn't mention."

"Wow, talk about a white knight."

"That's what I said." She shared a grin with her bestie as they moved on to cat-cow stretches. "Kell's been great, going above and beyond to fix whatever needs to be done even if it's not on Donald's list."

"Kell?" Rachel arched one dark eyebrow.

She shrugged, arching her back to stretch the muscles. "His friends call him Kell."

"Ooh, so you two are friends then?"

Glancing at Rachel under her arm, she took in her best friend's cheeky grin. She knew that look. Sadly, Rachel was about to be very disappointed.

"Get that thought right out of your head. He's a true-love hater."

Rachel frowned, moving into frog pose. "What does that mean?"

She shrugged, following into the position to stretch her hip flexors. "We were talking about the show the other day and he said *Romeo and Juliet* is a tragedy, not a romance."

Rachel lifted one shoulder. "Technically he's right."

She glared. "Not you too."

"Face it, babe. You've always been a romantic."

One of the reasons they worked as friends, but not lovers. Rachel was a realist. While she could handle Piper's romantic notions as a friend, she hadn't been able to deal with them as a girlfriend. A few weeks into their relationship they decided to call it off and be friends instead.

"But the play is one of Shakespeare's tragedies," Rachel went on.

"Whatever." Piper waved away the very logical point. "It doesn't matter. He said he doesn't date. He's not into labels."

"Ah, commitment phobia?"

Piper shrugged. Possibly, but she sensed it went deeper than that. Not like she'd ever find out. No sense in getting closer to someone who laid out their feelings on dating and relationships so clearly. She might be an optimist, but she was not going to jump into anything that was doomed from the start.

"Then he's not your Prince Charming," Rachel continued. "Maybe he could be a Prince Just for a Night or Two?"

Piper shook away the tempting thought. "You know I can't do that."

She'd tried casual hookups. It never worked. She was a heart-on-her-sleeve type of gal. Feelings always got involved, whether she wanted them to or not. She couldn't help it. Not once had she been with someone where it didn't turn into a relationship of at least nine months. Rachel was the only exception, and they turned into besties, which was another kind of loving relationship anyway.

"I'm sorry, babe. He sounded good for you."

She thought so too, which is why it sucked so much to have to see him every day. Temptation in a tool belt.

"And it's about time for you to move on from Larry the Loser." Rachel growled out the name, bitter and harsh.

Her best friend knew all about how her ex took all the money and ran. She didn't know Piper was living in the theater. It was too embarrassing to admit. Besides, she knew if she told, Rachel would insist she come stay with her and her girlfriend in their place. A five-hundred-square-foot studio apartment. No thank you. She was fine where she was as long as no one found out.

"I'll find someone, eventually." Just not Kell. A sad sigh left her.

"Well," Rachel said, moving up on her knees to stretch her arms. "I think that—"

The rest of her statement was interrupted by

a very loud curse and the sounds of tools being dropped. Piper sprang to her feet, jumped off the stage and rushed into the audience, up the stairs to where Kell was gripping one hand tightly to his chest.

"Kell! What happened?"

She knelt by his side, heart stopping in her chest as she spied dark red liquid seeping out from his clenched fist through his work glove.

"Damn carpet runner slipped and got me. Sliced clean through my glove." He shook his head. "Sorry about cursing. I'm fine."

"You're bleeding," she pointed out.

Kell released his fist, unclenching and pulling off his glove. She gasped at what he revealed. A four-inch slice ran from the bottom of his palm up to nearly his pinkie. Blood oozed from the cut, terrifying her with the sight.

"We need to get you to a hospital."

He huffed out a small laugh. "For a little cut? It's fine."

"You might need stitches," she insisted.

He shook his head. "The glove took the worst of it. I'll need some butterfly bandages at most."

Stubborn man! She glanced down at the carpet runner. Half of it was raised in the air. It looked like a snake, poised for another attack. There wasn't much blood on it, but the silver metal was speckled with dark brown rust spots.

"What about tetanus? That thing looks rusty. When was your last tetanus shot?"

Kell frowned, eyes narrowing in thought. "I guess it has been a while."

"That settles it. Hospital." Tetanus was no joke. "Let's go."

He blinked up at her as she stood, holding out her hand. "You don't have to take me. I can drive myself."

"With that hand? No. Safety first. I'm driving."

A small grin tugged at the corner of his lips. He nodded toward the stage where every single cast member was watching them with rapt attention. "What about your class?"

She shrugged. "This isn't a class. It's rehearsal for the show and Rachel can take over." She turned, using her stage voice to loudly call out. "Rachel, can you take over rehearsal? We have an emergency."

"Not an emergency," Kell grumbled. "Barely a scratch."

She rolled her eyes. Save her from stubborn men.

"Can do, Piper," Rachel answered, then told everyone on stage to follow her in warm-ups.

"There," she said, turning back to Kell and holding out her hand again. "That's settled, now I'm taking you to the hospital. Let's go, mister."

Kell grinned, the sight making her stomach flip-flop. She told her body to cool it. She was just helping. Like she would for anyone who got hurt in her proximity.

But when Kell slipped his uninjured hand into hers, allowing her to help him up, a sharp zing of heat and desire engulfed her. She quickly dropped his hand once he stood. Dang it. She really wished she could do casual hookups, but she knew herself better. One night in Kell's bed and she'd fall hard. Since the man didn't do forever, she'd be left with nothing but a broken heart and she wasn't sure how many more of those she could take.

CHAPTER NINE

THIS WAS RIDICULOUS.

Kell sat on the firm hospital bed. The paper stuff they used over the bed crinkled underneath him with any slight movement. It was sweet that Piper was worried about him, but this rush to the hospital had been entirely unnecessary. He could have wrapped the wound up, finished the workday and headed over to get a tetanus shot after.

"I don't think it needs any stitches," Dr. Walker said, examining his hand. "Surgical glue should be sufficient. You say you cut it on a piece of metal?"

"That's right." He nodded to the middle-aged Black man, who noted something on the computer next to the bed. "I was repairing a carpet runner. The edging trim slipped and got me clean through my glove."

Dr. Walker nodded. "And when was your last tetanus shot?"

"I'm afraid I can't remember, but I believe it was more than ten years ago."

The sound of clacking filled the room as the doctor typed something into the system. "I see.

Then you'll need a booster shot. Better to be safe when dealing with things like this."

He nodded his agreement, swearing he heard a soft "I told you so" from the side. He glanced over to where Piper was sitting in a chair against the wall. Her face held a smug look of vindication, but her eyes were filled with worry.

For him?

He wasn't sure how to feel about that. Usually, he was the one worrying about everyone else. It was a strange feeling having someone fret over him. He didn't know what to do with it.

"I've put it in the system. A nurse should be in soon to administer the shot and we'll get you all fixed up."

"Thank you, Doctor Walker."

Dr. Walker smiled at them both before heading out of the room. Silence filled the air. He could feel the energy thicken, heard the tapping of Piper's foot against the hard floor.

"It's okay," he said with a soft chuckle. "You can say it."

There was a beat of silence. Then.

"I told you so."

A squeak sounded as she rose from the chair and came over to stand in front of him. Concern marred her brow as she frowned.

"I told you this would need to be fixed."

Hoping to tease the worry from her eyes, he lifted one finger, pointing to his injured hand.

"Technically you said I would need stitches, but I don't."

Her eyes narrowed. "But you do need a tetanus shot. I was right about that."

He shrugged. "You got me there."

"Ha!" Now it was her turn to point. "Admit I was right about going to the hospital, just like I was right about the tacos."

He waved his uninjured hand in the air. "Eh, I still say I could have waited until I was done."

"And bleed all over everything?" Her eyes widened. "You can't be serious."

He wasn't. She had been right to stop work and head to the hospital right away, but the more he argued with her, the more the worry in her eyes turned to exasperation. He'd much rather she be annoyed with him than fear for him. He didn't want Piper to be stressed, especially over him. There was no need for anyone to worry over him. He could take care of himself.

"Why are men the most stubborn creatures on the planet?" She threw her hands up in exasperation. "I swear you could be drowning in a pool of quicksand a woman warned you about and you'd all insist it was nothing more than a child's sandbox. I can't believe…"

Her words trailed off as she stared at him, light dawning in her eyes.

"Wait a minute. Are you disagreeing with me as a distraction?"

Busted.

"You seemed worried," he said with a small shrug. "There's no need, I'm fine. And I noticed since we got here you looked…tense."

She grabbed a lock of hair, twisting the dark brown strands highlighted with streaks of blue around her finger as her eyes cast downward. "I don't like hospitals. They can be…overwhelming. The lights are always too bright and there's harsh chemical smells. Plus, the beeping of the machines and loud announcements over the speaker. It's quite the sensory overload."

"Then why did you insist on coming with me?" If she hated hospitals that much, why was she here?

She shrugged, refusing to look at him. "You couldn't drive yourself with that hand, and it happened at my theater so it's my responsibility."

Not even close. Donald owned the theater so any issue with his injury would fall on him. Irrelevant in this case anyway. This had been entirely his fault. A moment of carelessness. Besides, he was fine. A little glue, a small shot and he'd be right as rain.

"Thank you for coming," he said softly, realizing how hard this had been for her to do. "If you want to take off, I'm good now."

Her head snapped up, fingers dropping from her hair. "But how will you get back to your car? It's at the theater still."

They'd taken her car here. The thing was so old and worn down he was surprised it still worked.

"I can call a rideshare."

She shook her head. "No. I'm fine. You're almost done anyway. We're just waiting for the—"

Before she could finish her statement there was a knock on the door. It opened and the doctor came in, followed by a tall white man in nurse scrubs who looked so young Kell wondered if the guy graduated last week.

"Okay," Dr. Walker said, sitting on the round stool and wheeling it over to where Kell sat. "Let's get you fixed up and on your way."

The nurse held a tray with a variety of items on it. After the doctor washed his hands and put gloves on, he cleaned Kell's wound again. Next, he pressed the skin together as he moved the tube of surgical glue along the cut. Kell still maintained that he could have done this himself with a few butterfly bandages. The glue seemed like overkill. But the relieved smile on Piper's face as the doctor finished up was worth the fuss he decided.

"And now Brandon here will give you your shot," Dr. Walker said, standing. "I want you to keep the wound dry for the next forty-eight hours. After that you can shower, but no soaking the area. Pat dry and don't pick at the glue. It will dissolve on its own in a week or two. Keep an eye out for any sign of infection. If it appears red or starts oozing or you contract a fever, come back in right away, understand?"

He nodded. "Yes, sir."

"I'll leave you to it. You both have a better night."

Dr. Walker left and Brandon took his spot on the stool. The young man opened another alcohol wipe and cleaned a small spot on Kell's upper arm. Next, he reached for the small syringe on the silver tray. Kell heard Piper suck in a sharp breath. He glanced over at her to see her face go pale.

"Hey," he said, holding out his hand. "You okay?"

She grasped his hand tightly, nearly cutting off the circulation with her grip.

"I don't like needles."

He laughed in surprise. "Really? You have like a dozen tattoos."

She glanced down at the flowers cascading down her arm. "That's different."

"How?" He tugged her to the side, positioning his body so she had to focus on his face and couldn't see the nurse, needle poised above his arm.

"Tattoo needles are in that gun thing. You can't really see them. And after I get cool art forever."

"Fair point, but after a shot you get protection from diseases."

"I didn't say I didn't get them," she argued. "I said I don't like them and—"

"All done," Brandon announced, putting a bandage over the injection site. "I have a printout here with all the instructions the doctor told you. Feel free to give us a call if you have any questions and remember to look out for signs of infection. Y'all are free to go."

"Thank you, I will."

The nurse gathered the tray of supplies and left the room. Once they were alone again, Piper narrowed her eyes at him.

"You did it again, didn't you? With the tattoo needle stuff. You were trying to distract me?"

"Maybe." He squeezed her hand. "It worked, didn't it?"

A soft smile graced her face. "Thank you."

She squeezed back before releasing his hand and stepping back. "Should we get you back to your car?"

He nodded. "And you back to rehearsal."

Piper glanced at the clock on the wall. "It'll be over by now."

Damn. Now he felt terrible. He knew how important this show was to her. "I'm sorry for causing you to miss it."

She waved away his apology. "It's fine. Rachel can handle things for the night."

"Is she your assistant?"

"Assistant, best friend, best ex, and all-around angel."

"Best ex?" He tilted his head at the phrase. "Do you have a worst ex?"

She barked out a laugh that was in no way humor filled. "Only about a dozen of them. I don't have the best track record when it comes to dating."

Why on earth not? She was funny, smart, beautiful and talented. If he believed in love, he was sure he'd fall right at her feet. He must have looked confused, because Piper swallowed, cheeks pinkening as she explained.

"People find me charming at first, but then as time goes on, I guess the charm turns to annoyance. They think I'm putting on an act and then seem to get disappointed when it's like, no that's my real personality. The Manic Pixie Dream Girl problem."

"I'm sorry, what?"

She grabbed a lock of hair and twirled it again. "It's this theory I have. You know how the Manic Pixie Dream Girl character is always this quirky girl who does random things and has weird interests?"

He nodded. He wasn't a huge movie guy, but he'd seen enough to understand the concept.

"I think Manic Pixie Dream Girls are just autistically coded women. But in real life, the reality of our 'quirks' don't go away after a ninety minute movie run time. The allure quickly fades for a lot of people, and I turn from 'charming' to 'annoying' real quick."

He frowned, hating that she had to deal with that. Hating that people were so shallow and uninformed. Her theory made sense. It also made him angry. For her and every other person who had to deal with people treating them that way.

"I take it Rachel didn't find you annoying?" If she didn't, he couldn't imagine her being labeled the best ex.

"No, sadly we just realized we worked better as friends than girlfriends. To be honest, it's usually the guys I date who get annoyed with me when it turns out I'm not their quirky muse or whatever."

"Their loss," he grunted, angry at every single one of those idiots who had Piper in their arms and let her go. If he wasn't cursed by love, he'd snatch Piper up and never let her go.

She shrugged, clearly unable to see her worth thanks to the jerks of her past. He wished he could find every one of them and give them a lesson in manners.

"Should we head out?" he asked, desperate to change the topic and get that doleful look out of Piper's eyes.

"Yes, please. I am so ready to leave."

He rose from the hospital bed. His stomach cramped, a soft rumble sounding. Glancing at the clock, he frowned.

"It's past dinner." No wonder his stomach was pitching a fit. "Should we grab a bite before heading back? My treat."

Piper waved away his offer. "Oh, that's not necessary."

"I know, but I want to. Think of it as a thank-you for taking me to hospital."

She chuckled. "You mean *insisting* you go to the hospital."

"Hey, you were right."

"Naturally." She smiled.

He laughed, loving her charm. How could anyone find her annoying? Idiots.

"Plus, I owe you for the tacos," he added.

"Well, when you put it that way," she said, tapping her finger on her chin. "I supposed we could grab a bite."

A huge grin split his lips as they made their way to the door and out of the room. Spending more time alone with this woman was the very last thing he should do. They'd already agreed they were too different in the relationship department. They wanted different things, so starting anything was a recipe for disaster. And yet he couldn't stop this driving pull tugging at him whenever he so much as thought about her.

This was bad, he knew that.

Then why did it feel so right?

CHAPTER TEN

PIPER FOLLOWED KELL'S directions down the city streets. When he asked her where she wanted to go, she told him to pick. Decisions were a bit beyond her brain capacity right now. Hospitals were always unpleasant for her. Not only was she overwhelmed and her senses frazzled, but they also brought back memories of her emergency appendectomy in the sixth grade. Everything had turned out fine, but the experience had been far from pleasant and left a lasting bad memory for hospitals in general.

"The restaurant is on the right, just here," Kell said, pointing with his uninjured hand. "There's a lot you can park in after the building."

Thank goodness. Parking in Denver was a nightmare. Any place that had a lot downtown was prime real estate. Even the theater lacked in that area. Their tiny lot only held about a dozen cars. Thankfully the grocery store next door didn't mind if patrons parked in their lot for shows. She wished Donald would put a parking structure on their lot to hold more cars, but considering he'd only just agreed to the fixes she'd been asking for for years, she doubted that would ever happen.

"Yup, just turn in here," Kell said as they arrived.

Piper parked her car, glancing up at the side of the brick building adorned with a stunning mural of a large humpback whale swimming gracefully in the ocean. The letters of the restaurant's name swirled around in the water.

"The Blue Pearl. I've been wanting to try this place."

The seafood restaurant had recently opened, garnering great press. She'd been meaning to try it as she loved seafood but was unfortunate to live in a landlocked state where it wasn't a go-to delicacy.

"Glad I picked it then." Kell smiled at her. "Shall we?"

They got out of the car and headed toward the front doors. It was midweek, past the dinnertime rush, but the new restaurant was still packed. Her stomach rumbled, nerves rising again as they had to push through a crowded entryway to make it up to the host stand in order to put their names on the list.

"Kellen Thorson, two," Kell said, smiling pleasantly at the white woman with dark hair slicked back in a low ponytail standing at the podium.

The hostess's smile was tight as she tapped away on the tablet in her hand. Clearly it was a stressful and busy night. Piper could relate. She'd done her time in the serving trenches years ago. It had been awful. People were the worst when it came to eating out. In her opinion, everyone should be required to work a customer service job for at least two years so they knew what it was like. Then maybe there wouldn't be so many rude customers making people cry just for doing their job.

"I'm sorry, we have a forty-five-minute wait time, but—oh." The woman blinked as she stared at the screen in front of her. "Mr. Thorson. Yes, right this way."

"Thank you."

Thank you? What? What about the forty-five-minute wait?

Piper frowned, confusion pushing out the frazzled energy as Kell grabbed her hand and followed the hostess. The woman weaved around the tables in the large main room. Piper caught bits of conversation from the tables they passed, but what she really wanted to know was what the heck just happened. How did they skip the line?

They finally stopped near the very back of the large room. A small booth table sat in a corner, slightly secluded from the rest of the dining area. The high walls of the booth surrounding three-quarters of the table provided a barrier from the sights and sounds from the rest of the room.

"Here you are," the hostess said, motioning to the table. "Your server will be right with you."

"Thank you." Kell nodded, motioning for Piper to sit first.

Still confused over what was going on, she slid into the booth, breathing a sigh of relief when the noisy clatter of conversation and eating dimmed. Kell slid in on the other side of the booth, picking up the menu the hostess had left on the table for them and perusing it.

She waited exactly three seconds before getting to the point.

"What was that?"

Kell tilted his menu down, blinking at her with confusion. "Huh?"

"That." She waved a hand to where the hostess had just been.

"I'm not following."

Really? Or was he acting bewildered on purpose?

"This is a brand-new restaurant," she started. "It's been featured in Westword, on the news, even on that fancy cuisine blog Rachel follows. You saw the crowd up front and the hostess said there was a forty-five-minute wait time. But you give your name, and *poof*, suddenly we have a table right away."

"I always have a table right away here."

He said it like it was the most normal thing in the world. Like it wasn't weird that he had "a table" at one of the hottest restaurants in the city.

"And how did you manage that? Did you sell your soul or something?"

He chuckled, putting the menu down and placing his forearms on the table. He leaned across the tabletop. She mimicked his movement until their faces were inches apart.

"I'd tell you," he whispered in a low, seductive voice. "But then I'd have to kill you."

The corner of his lips ticked up in a playful smile. She grabbed her menu and lightly smacked him on the shoulder. The black cardstock made a small thunking sound as it struck its mark.

"Hey!" He laughed, sitting back against the booth's back. "I'm injured, you can't hit an injured man."

"I hit your uninjured side and you're being willfully obtuse! Now tell me why you can waltz into the hottest restaurant in the city and have a standing reservation."

He shrugged, picking up his menu again and scanning it as he answered her.

"My brothers and I…helped the owner with this place so he made sure to have this back table ready for us whenever we wanted. The staff also uses it if we're not here."

"You guys did contracting work here?"

He shrugged. "Among other things."

That sounded…odd, but then again, she knew all about tit for tat among business owners. She had her own "I scratch your back, you scratch mine" deals with a few places. Like the yoga supply store that gave her students a discount or the lighting company that got free show tickets in exchange for new gels and bulbs. You had to hustle to stay in business these days.

She picked up her menu again to glance over the selection. Her eyes nearly fell out of her head as she saw the prices. Holy cow! Nothing was under thirty dollars. Not even the salads. What in the world could be in a salad to make it thirty-five dollars?

"My treat, remember?" Kell said, giving her a knowing look.

He must have seen the sticker shock on her face.

She leaned in close again, not wanting to offend any of the workers should they pass by and hear. "Kell, this place is ridiculously expensive. I can't let you cover my meal."

It was too much, even for friends.

He waved away her protest. "It's fine. You got the tacos, remember?"

"The tacos were six bucks. Just breathing in this place will cost you sixty."

He laughed softly, placing his menu back on the table and staring at her with a soft warmth in his bright blue eyes.

"Piper, I promise you, I can afford it."

"How?" Her eyes roamed over the prices again, hoping she'd misread the totals. Nope, still ridiculously expensive. "I know what it's like to be a small business owner, Kell. I don't know how much contractors make, but I do know what a tightwad Donald is, and I can guarantee you he's not paying you splurge-at-seafood-restaurant prices."

She desperately wanted to eat here, but not if it meant putting Kell's finances in harm's way. Her finances being what they were, she would never do that to another person. A thought occurred to her.

"Does the owner give you a discount on food too?" Seemed like overkill for doing his job, but maybe Kell and his brothers hadn't charged the guy at all for their work and this was how he paid them back.

"No." Kell shook his head. He focused on his menu, refusing to look at her. His brow furrowed. "My family…is comfortable."

She snorted. "That's something rich people say when they don't want to admit they're rich. You're a trust fund baby then?"

He scowled. "No. Not exactly. My family's businesses do very well."

"'Do very well,'" she muttered under her breath. "More rich-person talk. How rich are we talking? Millionaire? Billionaire?"

"Didn't anyone ever tell you it's not polite to discuss finances?"

Checking out the meal options, she lifted one shoulder in a small shrug. "Yes, but no one has ever been able to explain why."

Saying something was a rule meant nothing

without the reasoning behind it. She never understood why people thought it was okay to just state something without explaining why. An old therapist told her that was a trait of her autism. She considered it common sense. Something a lot of people lacked, in her opinion.

Kell stared for a moment, tilting his head slightly as the corner of his mouth moved up in a knowing smile. "Do you have a problem with rich people, Piper?"

"Only when they hoard their wealth at the expense of others suffering," she answered truthfully. "In my experience, most rich people are selfish jerks."

He laughed. "Knowing a lot of them, I have to agree. But I hope I'm the exception to the rule. Yes, my family has money, but our parents also insisted we work hard and give back. Which is why my brothers and I run a housing charity. We buy abandoned properties and fix them up, then we donate those houses to unhoused families in need and take care of the property tax as well."

Her heart melted a little at his reveal. "You do?"

He nodded. "We've housed nearly fifty families since we started the charity."

Well, shoot! She'd been a little excited to find out he was rich. It was something she could use to combat her rising desire for this man. If he was a trust fund baby, she could put him in the category of rich snob who didn't care about those around them. But it sounded like Kell and his brothers cared deeply about helping those in need. Dang it! Why did he have to be a love hater? Every new fact she learned about him set him firmly in her Mr. Right box.

Every one except the big one.

He didn't believe in happily-ever-after.

Frustration at her conundrum mounting, she pushed it aside and focused on what Kell had revealed about his charity work.

"That's amazing, Kell. I guess that means you're not a completely horrible rich person. You're more like Ebenezer Scrooge, post ghost haunting."

He laughed, the rich, deep sound vibrating from her chest all the way down to her toes. Warming up all the places in between.

"Thank you. I try to keep Christmas in my heart all year round."

She laughed along with him, glad they could remain friendly even as she started to realize how different they were. When their server came to take their orders, she tried to get away with ordering the cheapest thing on the menu.

"Piper," Kell said, seeming to stare into her very soul. "Please, order what you want."

She sighed, reminding herself this man was apparently loaded—or his parents were anyhow—and he could afford it. Far be it from her to argue with a man who wanted to spoil her. It didn't happen often…or at all really. She might as well take advantage of it while she could.

Taking a breath, she picked up her menu, eyes drawn to the entrée that had been making her mouth water for the past ten minutes. "I'll have the filet minion with the king crab legs. Medium please."

The server nodded. "And for you, sir?"

Kell handed over his menu, smiling at her. "Sounds delicious. I'll have the same."

"Excellent choice. Any wine for the table?"

Kell deferred to her. She shook her head.

"I'm fine with water, thank you."

She had to drive them back to the theater. One glass of wine wouldn't impair her abilities, but she was worried about lowering her defenses around this charming man. She already knew it was a bad idea to start anything. Add alcohol into the mix, and her brain would forget why he was all wrong for her.

CHAPTER ELEVEN

"HOLY COW, DON'T TELL the taco truck, but I think this is the most delicious thing I've ever eaten."

Kell chuckled, popping a bite of the tender, juicy meat into his mouth and chewing before swallowing. "Your secret is safe with me."

She laughed when he mimed zipping his lips. She was right. This food was amazing. He knew that because he came to eat here every week since it had opened. Guilt wormed its way into his gut, souring the delicious meal as he recalled his earlier lie. Not a lie really, more of an omission. While it was true he and his brothers did a bit of work on this building when the owner bought it—they put in a top-of-the-line cooktop—that wasn't the only reason the Thorson brothers had their own standing reservation.

He had been the real estate agent responsible for finding and securing the purchase for the owner. He'd been so grateful for the amazing deal he'd promised the brothers a table whenever they wanted.

It wasn't that he wanted to lie to Piper. But he

worried if she knew he was also one of the top property agents in the Denver Metro area, she'd get suspicious and start asking about Donald and his plans for the theater. Every fiber of his being wanted to shout out the secret he was keeping from her. It wasn't fair. She deserved to know. She deserved time to make plans. Damn Donald for making him sign that unscrupulous NDA. He never should have taken this job.

But then I wouldn't have met her.

He glanced across the table, watching as Piper dipped a piece of crab into the rich, melty butter. Her eyes lit up with hunger as she brought the bite to her mouth. Eyes closing, she let out a small moan of delight as she bounced up and down in her seat. Pure joy radiating off every inch of her. All from the simple act of eating delicious food. His body tightened with need as his heart swelled.

What was this woman doing to him?

"I can't believe you get to eat here whenever you want." Piper's eyes opened. "I bet this spot gets you a lot of action with the ladies." She waggled her eyebrows but then frowned. "Wait, do you even go on dates? I'm not sure how your deal works."

"My 'deal'?"

"Yeah." She waved a hand in his direction. "Your whole 'love doesn't exist' deal. That must make it hard to date. Do you date or do you just hook up? No judgment, just trying to figure it out."

She had certainly judged him a lot the other day

when he said *Romeo and Juliet* was a tragedy, not a romance.

"Yes, I date." He smiled softly at her, grabbing his glass and drinking a sip of water before continuing. "But I make it very clear with the women I go out with that I don't do long-term. And to be completely honest, besides my brothers, you're the only other person who has eaten here with me."

She paused, forkful of roasted carrots halfway to her lips. Her mouth dropped open in surprise. "I am?"

He nodded. Shoving the bite into her mouth, she didn't say anything else. Her brow furrowed as if she was confused by this whole situation. *Join the club.* He had no idea what was going on. His brain knew they were incompatible—they wanted different things in life, they came from different backgrounds, he was withholding a giant secret from her. But the rest of him screamed at him to drop his silly "no dating" rule and take a chance on what he and Piper could be.

I can't.

Even if he wanted to, the curse would ensure it ended in disaster yet again.

"So why don't you date?" Piper popped an elbow on the table and placed her chin in her hand. "If you don't mind me asking."

A heavy sigh left him. Pushing away his plate, he leaned back against the padded booth.

"I'm cursed."

Her eyes widened. "Cursed?"

He didn't like talking about his odd past, but she deserved to know why he was so adamant about no forever.

"My high school girlfriend and I dated for four years. We were perfect together. Got along great, had chemistry. I thought we were headed toward marriage, but then our second year of college she told me the spark died. We were both stressed with classes, and I admit our relationship had veered more toward a close friendship than a relationship. We broke up but remained friends."

"That's nice," Piper noted. "Unless she broke up with you because she'd been cheating on you?"

"No, it wasn't like that. However, she did meet a guy two months after we broke up. They fell madly in love and were married within a year."

Her jaw dropped wide. "Woah! That's fast. Are they still together? Do you know?"

He nodded. Weirdly, he kept in touch with all his exes. That was part of the problem. "They are. Happily married with three rug rats."

"I'm sorry. I don't see how that makes you cursed—"

"She wasn't the only one," he interrupted her. "My next four girlfriends were the same exact thing. We'd date for a while, everything was going great. Chemistry fizzled. We broke up amicably and then *boom*, they'd find the love of their life right after me. I'm like some weird good luck love charm for everyone."

"Everyone except you," Piper said softly, understanding and sympathy filling her eyes.

He nodded. "A charm for them, a curse for me."

"I don't know that I believe in curses, but I can see how that would make someone resistant to relationships. But it's kind of sad you've given up on love. Love is the greatest thing in the world."

"Says the woman who admits she has a lot of bad exes." He raised one eyebrow. "Sounds like we have similar problems in the love department."

She waved away his rebuttal. "I know I've struck out in the relationship department a lot, but that doesn't mean I'm giving up. My grandparents were married for fifty years. When my grandfather looked at my grandmother, it was as if no one else was in the room. You could feel the love radiating off them. They passed within a day of each other because my grandpa couldn't live without Grandma. That's the kind of love I'm looking for."

Wow. That sounded amazing. His parents' marriage was pretty standard. They didn't argue, but they weren't overly expressive with each other. No wonder Piper was such a hopeless romantic with an example like her grandparents.

"Aren't you worried about being lonely forever?" she asked.

He shrugged. "I've got my family, friends, job

and my charity work. There's love in all of that enough for me."

She remained silent, finishing off her meal to the sounds of the dinner rush dying down. Their server came back to take their plates and leave the bill. Piper tried to protest him paying, but he insisted, seeing as how she drove him to the hospital, and he'd ruined her rehearsal.

They got into her car and drove back to the theater, chatting about her time in a traveling circus. He loved the way her face lit up when she talked about her aerials. The passion she had for the art was contagious. It almost made him want to agree to their silly bet and get up in an apparatus.

Almost.

"Are you sure you're okay driving home?" Piper asked for the fourth time.

Kell chuckled. They were sitting in her car just outside the theater. Dinner had been amazing. Not only the food but the company too. He hated to go home, but it was the best thing—for both of them.

"I'll be fine. It doesn't even hurt anymore." He raised his bandaged hand and waved it around to prove it. "You get home safe. How far away do you live?"

She bit her lip, head swiveling away as she fiddled with the air vent by the side of the dash. "Oh, I'm super close. Don't worry about me. You take care of that hand and remember what the doctor said about signs of infection."

He chuckled softly. "Yes ma'am."

She rolled her eyes, but her lips curved into a smile. "Thank you for dinner. It was delicious."

"My pleasure."

The air in the car thickened as they stared at each other. He could feel the heat radiating off her body, see the desire darken her eyes. His hand rose of its own accord, fingers gently brushing her cheek. Her lips parted and a small whimper of need escaped them. Longing pulled at him to lean in closer and cover those lips with his own. Taste their sweetness.

But Piper pulled back.

Sadness filled her gaze as she stared back at him. "Good night, Kell."

He blinked, the spell broken as the reality of their situation reared its ugly head. Gracing her with a soft, sad smile of his own, he opened the car door and got out.

"Bye, Piper."

He got into his car and drove to his house. It was an older home he and his brothers had restored a few years ago. He lived in the heart of the city along with Cash while Mal had a place out in the mountains just outside Denver. As he unlocked his door, mind still preoccupied with Piper and how he'd almost kissed her like a fool, he didn't even notice the man sitting on his couch.

"Hey, dude."

Kell let out a shout of surprise that turned into

a curse when he recognized the man with similar dark hair and features to his, sitting there, eating his chips.

"Dammit, Cash. What did I say about coming into my home and eating my food when I'm not here?"

"*Mi casa es su casa?*" Cash shrugged.

"Nice try, but you failed high school Spanish. Get your dirty feet off my coffee table."

"Whoa, who shoved a claw hammer up your butt today, big brother?"

He growled, a headache forming, pounding away at his temple. Younger siblings had the worst timing. It was like a curse. Cash rose from the couch and disappeared into the kitchen. He returned a moment later with two beers. Popping off the tops, he offered one to Kell.

"Spill it. Not the beer," Cash hurried to clarify. "Whatever is bothering you."

A heavy sigh filled Kell's chest as he sunk down onto the soft cushions of the couch. After taking a fortifying sip of his beer, he launched into everything from meeting Piper to their time hanging out, tonight's injury and dinner, and their discussion.

"Ah, you told her about your ridiculous 'curse' theory." Cash nodded.

Kell scowled at his brother. "It's not ridiculous. It's true. Once or twice, I'd say it's a coincidence, but five times? It's a pattern."

"Patterns can be broken." Cash shrugged. "If

you like this woman, you should go for it. Maybe she's the one to break the curse or whatever fairy-tale nonsense you believe."

He shook his head. Cash didn't get it. Of course the middle Thorson brother, the playboy dreamer who fell in love every five seconds and fell out of love just as easily would think it's that simple. It wasn't. His curse wasn't the only issue here.

"What happens when she finds out Donald is selling the theater?"

Cash paused, beer halfway to his mouth. He winced, lowering the bottle. "Yeah. That does put a kink in things. She's gonna be mad, I bet."

More than mad. Furious, betrayed, scared…the last one worried him the most. Where would she go after she lost the theater? Would her business survive? What about all the people who benefited from her aerial classes?

"Maybe you can help her find a new theater?" Cash suggested.

He shook his head. Denver was a large city, but it wasn't like there were a bunch of vacant theaters just lying around waiting for tenants. Plus… "I doubt she'll want to talk to me after she finds out I'm the one selling the place."

"You could tell her," Cash suggested.

"You know I can't." As it was a family-run business, all the brothers knew every detail of their contracts. "If I tell Piper Donald is planning on selling the place and not renewing her lease, he can fire me and sue us. That puts Helping Homes at risk. I can't do that."

Their charity was too important. It helped so many people. He couldn't risk all of them for her… no matter how badly he wanted to.

"Damn," Cash swore. "That is a rock and a hard place."

Tell me about it. He was screwed no matter what he did. What he figured would be an easy repair-and-sell job had turned into the biggest mess of his life, and for once he had no answers on how to solve it.

CHAPTER TWELVE

"If you stare at that man any harder your eyes are going to pop out of your head," Rachel whispered with a small chuckle.

Piper whipped her head around to glare at her supposed best friend. "I wasn't staring."

"You were, babe. Hard. Like mask dropping, unaware-of-your-surroundings staring."

One of the kids let out a shout of glee, diverting Piper's attention. She smiled as she watched the groups of eight-to-eleven-year-old children spin to their hearts' content in the aerial slings she'd hung for sensory class today. They were enjoying free play for the last ten minutes of class.

"I wasn't staring," she insisted again. "I was simply checking to see how he was doing today with work. The man was injured on the job. I don't want to…get sued."

A pathetic excuse for what she'd actually been doing—ogling those forearms out on full display—and one she knew Rachel would in no way buy.

"Yeah, I'm not buying it."

See?

"Besides." Rachel crossed her arms over her chest and arched one eyebrow. "Donald is the one who hired Kell, so he'd be the one to get sued. Not you."

She had a point.

"Ms. Piper, look what I can do!"

The high-pitched call of excitement drew her gaze as Kelsey, a sweet nine-year-old girl with fire-red hair and a million freckles gracing her pale face flipped upside down in a mermaid-tail position and spin herself so fast Pipe's stomach started to turn. The joyful cries of happiness from the young girl made her heart swell.

This is why she loved her job. Not just to share her love of aerial arts, but for kids like Kelsey. When the young girl came to her first class, she'd been quiet, refusing to talk to anyone, almost fearful. But when she saw the other kids happily playing, receiving grace during a meltdown, and being allowed to be their enthusiastic authentic selves in her class, Kelsey had opened up. Piper understood that all too well. So many times as a child she'd been told to be quieter, calm down, stop acting so weird.

She always found it odd that society considered excitement and joy in something "weird." It took her years to realize the problem had never been her being too much. The problem lay with those who wanted to dim her light. She vowed to never make herself quieter or more palatable for others and she tried to instill that in these kiddos too.

"Great job, Kelsey!"

The young girl let out a shrieking giggle, which two of the kids echoed until the class was a fit of boisterous innocent laughter.

"Oops, now he's staring at you," Rachel said.

Piper's head moved of its own volition to where Kell was finishing up work in the audience. Heat burned her cheeks as she saw he was indeed staring at her with a warm smile on his handsome face. That smile should be illegal. She swore one day it was going to give her a heart attack.

Rachel laughed softly. "You both have it so bad."

"We do not," she protested, averting her gaze to focus on the kids again. "And even if we did, it's hopeless. I told you already."

"Yeah, yeah. He doesn't believe in love or dating." Rachel waved a hand in the air. "And you're not a hookup girl. But people can change."

"Ask permission, Caleb," Piper shouted to one of the boys who tried to grab another's sling and spin him. Giving a portion of her attention to Rachel, she asked, "You think I can change into a hookup queen?"

A sputter of laughter left Rachel's lips. "Queen? No, hun, you're too much of a romantic to ever be a hookup queen, but you might like it if you try it."

Now it was her turn to give an incredulous laugh. "I have tried it, and it resulted in a whirlwind relationship where he left town in the middle of the night." Leaving her homeless, but she hadn't shared that part with Rachel.

"Oh, right." Rachel's eyes darkened. "Loser."

Larry had been a loser. Of the highest degree. She would forever be embarrassed she let her romantic notions tip her over the edge with that man. Her quest to find a love like her grandparents' had caused her to pick some real duds. She needed to be smarter about picking partners, less emotional. Another reason she needed to ignore this incessant pull she felt toward Kell. On paper they were all wrong for each other.

"Then maybe Kell will change," Rachel offered. "You can be the one to open his heart and help him believe in true love."

How Piper wished that were true, but after hearing his reasoning last night she doubted anyone would ever get him to believe he wasn't cursed by love. Such a silly notion, but it was hard to argue with the facts. One partner finding forever love after a breakup was normal. Two was a coincidence. But five? She didn't know how to dispute that.

"I don't think anyone can." A heavy sigh left her as she glanced over at Kell sanding down the area he'd uncovered yesterday in anticipation of the new carpet runner he said was coming.

"That's too bad, because it appears plenty of people want to try."

She glanced at Rachel, who tilted her head to the side of the stage where the group of parents stood, waiting for the kids. Usually, the parents were busy taking pictures of the kids in the apparatuses, but today a number of the moms and a few of the dads were staring at Kell. Interest in their eyes. A dark wave of jealousy soured her gut. Ridiculous. She knew a few of those parents were single, and even the ones who weren't had every right to appreciate the handsome handyman. Being partnered didn't mean you stopped finding people attractive. And boy oh boy was Kell attractive. She didn't blame a single one of them, but she also couldn't stop the red-hot rage burning inside at the thought of Kell taking one of them home.

And that right there was why she couldn't pursue anything with Kell. Casual did not work for her. She didn't like sharing, and the thought of Kell hooking up with someone else while he was seeing her…no, she couldn't handle that.

"Hey, Piper." A rich, deep voice called her name.

She turned to see Kell standing at the base of the stage. He placed his forearms on the stage floor and leaned over, neck craning as he smiled up at her.

"Hi. Done for the day?"

He nodded. "Yeah. The new carpet won't get here until tomorrow and I don't want to start a new project until this one is finished, so I'm headed out."

It was nearly dinnertime anyway. Made sense. She was planning on calling it quits herself as this was her last class of the day.

"You ever thought of being on one of those fix-it-up shows, Kell?" Rachel asked, tilting her head toward the side of the stage where the parents stood. "You seem to have a rapt audience already."

Kell laughed, the sound tinged with discomfort. "Eh, not for me. Showing off for the camera is more my brother Cash's style."

Seeing his discomfort struck a chord in Piper. She hated when people stared at her. Though usually for her it was because she was acting in a way that wasn't considered "normal." She moved her body, crouching down to block Kell from view and to save his poor neck from staring up so far.

"What time will the carpet be delivered tomorrow?"

"Bright and early. I should be here around eight, if that's okay with you?"

She nodded. There weren't any classes until ten, so his load in would be uninterrupted. She made a mental note to be up and ready for the day as if she'd already gotten here early. Though, with each passing day, her "spy for Donald" notion was seemingly sillier and sillier. She couldn't imagine sweet, honest Kell lying to her about his true intentions here. True, she'd been fooled by people before, but judging by his action, all the work he'd put in, all the times he listened to her and took her suggestions, he was the real deal. A simple contractor here to work on the theater. Whatever reason made Donald finally hire him she might never know, but she was grateful.

"That works. See you tomorrow, Kell."

"Until tomorrow, Piper."

He smiled, the sight nearly knocking her off her crouched feet. A deadly weapon, that smile.

"Bye, Rachel," he added with a small wave.

"See ya round, Kell."

He turned to leave, getting exactly two feet before a few of the kids shouted, "Bye, Mr. Fix It Man!"

Kell laughed, turning and waving at all the kids. "Keep spinning, kids, but no puking."

A chorus of giggles erupted onstage as the kids spun faster, trying to do exactly what Kell warned them not to.

Thankfully no one lost their lunch. Class ended with the kids happily dizzy and handed off to their parents. Rachel asked if Piper wanted to go to dinner, but she declined. All she really wanted was a hot shower and a good night's sleep.

If that night of sleep included naughty dreams about a certain handyman, she wouldn't say no to that either. Seemed like the only way she could have Kell was in her dreams.

Once everyone was gone and the theater was locked up, she went to her room. Tossing her clothes in her hamper, she wrapped a towel around herself, grabbed her shower caddy filled with shampoo, conditioner and bodywash, and headed to the locker room. Kell hadn't addressed the water heater issue yet, but there was always enough hot water for one twenty-minute shower. She longed for a good forty-five-minute steam session, but that would have to wait.

After she soaped up and rinsed, Piper grabbed her towel and ran it over her hair, getting the excess water out. Next, she dried off as best she could then wrapped the towel around her, securing it.

"Oh, shoot." She frowned, realizing she forgot the cotton T-shirt she used to wrap her hair up in after a shower to prevent frizz. "Dang it."

Her head was all over the place lately. She blamed a handsome handyman who thought he was cursed. Such a silly notion, but not unfounded. If only there was some way she could convince him. She grabbed her shower caddy and started toward her room. As she left the locker room and headed toward the small staircase where her secret room sat, she heard a noise.

Pausing, she held her breath, listening. Silence filled the back of the stage. The muted sounds of traffic filtered in through the windows, but nothing from inside. Had she imagined it?

She shook her head. "I must be tired."

Staring down at the floor so as not to step on anything, Piper started to make her way again through the darkness of the backstage. She was about three feet from the stairs when suddenly she saw a looming shadow two feet in front of her. Letting out a bloodcurdling scream, she hurled her shower caddy at it. The bottles went flying from the plastic bin, crashing to the floor with a thud and splat as one opened and soapy contents oozed out. The shadow ducked.

"Piper?" The shadow spoke with an achingly familiar voice.

"K…Kell?"

The shadow took a step forward into a small beam of light from a high window. The full moon illuminated his handsome and confused face.

"What are you doing here?" Kell asked.

Oh no! The jig was up.

CHAPTER THIRTEEN

DAMMIT, HE SCARED her again. He had to stop doing that. It would help if he knew she was going to be at the theater when no one was supposed to be here. Seriously, why was she here?

"What are you doing here?" She echoed his question back at him.

He lifted his tool bag.

"I forgot my tools." Not the first time his ADHD made him forget something important and had him turning around. "I'm sorry I scared you, but I didn't think anyone would be here. What are you doing here?"

Her mouth popped open, but no words came out.

The shock of finding her in the dark abating, he finally noticed what she was wearing…or more accurately, what she wasn't wearing. "And why are you in a towel?"

Heat scorched his body at the sight. Tiny drops of water ran down her bare arms, sliding amongst the colorful flowers inked on her skin like a beautiful garden. Her dark hair, hung in wet, messy tendrils around her bare face. The faded cotton towel wrapped around her came to her mid-thighs, revealing even more brilliant blooms cascading down her legs. She reminded him of one of those flower nymphs in a fairy-tale book of Greek Mythology his mother read him as a kid. Beautiful and magical.

Piper's cheeks flamed red. Her head ducked down, hand flying to the knot on the towel, gripping it tight.

"I was taking a shower. Obviously."

Obviously. He got that from the dripping water, the shower caddy she threw at him and the lack of clothing. That last one he was struggling with most. His body tightened with need, the desire for this woman he'd been fighting rising to the top, ready to explode. But he pushed it down. Clearly something was wrong if Piper was here taking a shower in the dark. His baser hormones could chill. He wasn't a creep. He was a grown man. He would control himself.

"I can see that, but why? Why are you showering here and not at home?"

Silence filled the air. He watched Piper's lips roll in, eyes darting side to side. He smelled the lie even before she spoke it.

"The hot water in my apartment is on the fritz. My landlord hasn't fixed it yet. Guess scummy landlords are everywhere, right?"

Her laughter fell flat. He didn't join in. One thing Kell had always been able to do was spot when someone was lying. His brothers hated it growing up. None of his exes had liked it either. Wasn't his fault he was a human lie detector. It came in handy a lot. Like now. Something was wrong. He needed her to tell him so he could help. Desperation pulled at him. He had to do something. The waves of anxiety pouring off her alarmed him.

"Piper."

"What?" She scowled at him, refusing to meet his eyes, defiance stiffening her spine. "I needed a shower and prefer them hot to cold, okay? I was just headed home after."

"Like that?"

"Of course not. I was gonna change."

"Why didn't you change in the locker room where the showers are?" Something about this whole setup smelled fishy. "Why are you backstage in nothing but a towel?"

A small hint of humor ticked up the corner of her mouth as she finally looked at him.

"I've been backstage in far less."

What now?

"This is the theater, Kell. Sometimes you have to do a quick change. Finish one piece and you're in the one after the next? Looks like you're stripping offstage and slipping into your next costume and you better do it in less than five minutes because our riggers are fast. We set up a privacy screen for those who want it, but a lot of us just change in the open. It's so quick it's not like anyone notices or cares. Unless you miss your cue."

Huh. He couldn't say he knew what that was like at all. With his realty work he was always dressed in the finest suits, tailored specifically for him. When he did construction work it was jeans, T-shirts and flannels. There's been a time or two in the hot sun where he and the crew had stripped off their shirts to cool down, but in his line of work no one got naked in front of each other.

The theater was an odd place.

Still, her reasoning didn't answer his question. He knew avoidance when he heard it. If she thought she could shock him into dropping this, she was sorely mistaken.

"Piper, what is going on?"

"Nothing," she insisted. "I just…forgot…something out here and was coming to get it and then you came out of the shadows like a freaking vampire and scared the life out of me. Again! Seriously, you need to stop sneaking around the theater at odd hours. I'm gonna have to put a bell around your neck or something."

Her accusatory grumbles were adorable, but he also saw them for what they were. A distraction tactic. She didn't want to tell him why she was here in the middle of the night taking a shower and wandering around backstage naked. He got that, he did, but if she was in some kind of trouble, he wanted—no—he *needed* to help her.

"Never been one for wearing jewelry," he teased, trying to lighten the mood and ease her worry. "Hazard of the job if it gets caught on a tool. Ever heard of degloving?"

A shudder vibrated her bare shoulders. "Unfortunately, yes. Fine, no bell, but you should at least shout or announce your presence or something."

Announce his presence when he was walking into a building that was supposed to be empty? Something inside his mind clicked. Both times he'd surprised Piper, he assumed no one would be here. The first time because Donald told him. Logical to think the landlord wouldn't know the exact schedule of the tenant. He could chalk that one up to a simple mistake. But tonight. He left knowing her last class of the night was ending. He assumed she'd be going home, just like him.

Both times she was supposed to be at home, she was here.

Dread filled the pit of his stomach. He did not like the road his thoughts were traveling. As much as he wanted to blurt out his suspicions, he knew it would be a bad idea. Piper could be stubborn, he'd learned. Better for her to trust him enough to share. Now he just had to figure out a way to make her feel safe enough to do exactly that.

"I'm sorry I scared you," he started, because it was true. The very last thing he ever wanted to do was cause her stress, and it felt like he couldn't stop doing just that. "I should have announced myself, but I assumed you'd gone home. We all know what assuming makes us."

A small smile curved her lips at his joke. "Did you just call me an as—"

"No," he rushed to say. "Just me, you are an Anthousai."

Her face scrunched up. "A what?"

Oops! He hadn't meant to say that out loud. It slipped. Those flowers had hypnotized him, causing his brain to short-circuit. The words flew from his mouth without thought.

"A flower nymph. It's from Greek mythology. I had this picture book on Greek mythology as a kid. My mom read it to me every night. I was obsessed with the artwork. It was beautiful. Like oil painting but printed on the page and somehow the texture of the art still came through."

She arched one eyebrow, clearly not following him.

"Never mind, not important. Anyway, there were these flower nymphs, minor goddesses called Anthousai or Anthusa sometimes. Protectors of the flowers. They had flowers growing all over them and your tattoos made me think of it." He waved a hand at her arms and legs. "Silly, I know."

Her face softened. A sheen of moisture glossed her deep brown eyes. She blinked it away as a soft pink blush rose on her cheeks. "It's not silly. In fact, I think it's the nicest thing anyone has ever said to me. No one has ever compared me to a goddess before."

Then people were idiots. Piper far surpassed any goddess ever known. She was beautiful, smart, brave, talented and a million other amazing things he couldn't hope to put a name to if he had a hundred years to decipher. Some lucky person was going to get to spend forever with this amazing woman. He'd give every bit of his wealth if that someone could be him.

But the curse.

He knew if he started something with Piper it would end up like every other relationship he had. It hurt seeing his past girlfriends find their one true loves right after being with him, but he'd gotten over it. Mostly. If he had Piper and lost her... it would destroy him.

Better to never have her at all and save himself the heartbreak.

Not to mention he had a part in her losing her business. A fact she still had no idea about.

Damn this entire situation!

"Flowers make me happy." Piper gazed down at the vibrant ink adorning her skin. "They're so beautiful and they contribute so much to the ecosystem. They provide nourishment and homes for so many different insects and animals. Each one has a unique scent and purpose. They live such short lives compared to other plants, but they're tenacious. The winter may drive them underground, but every spring they pop back up, filling the world with beauty and hope."

Her fingers gently traced down her arm, sliding amongst the garden she'd created. He longed to follow that path.

"I started with this daisy here." She pointed to a faded pink daisy just below her right shoulder. "I got it when I got my first contract with a traveling circus. Daisies symbolize new beginnings. After that I just kept adding. You know what they say about tattoos—you can't have just one."

He chuckled. "I think that's potato chips."

She laughed softly along with him. As much as he hated to ruin the lightened mood, he knew it was time to press.

"Piper," he said gently. "What is going on? Why are you here so late? Are you in trouble?"

Silence filled the air around them. She stared at him, eyes focused on his with such intensity. Finally, she blinked, ducking her head.

"Okay." Her voice was the barest of whispers in the darkness that surrounded them. "I'll show you, but you have to swear not to tell anyone."

Cold dread crawled up his spine at her ominous words.

"Promise me, Kell."

He wanted to, but he couldn't promise to stay quiet if she was in danger.

"Kell?"

"I promise."

She nodded, smiling, but her smile fell when he continued. "As long as keeping your secret doesn't put you in danger."

She processed his words, face blank for a beat before her smile returned. "There's that white knight again. I swear I'm not in any danger. Just… in a bit of a low spot right now."

The knot in his chest eased at her words.

"Come on," she said, turning and heading up the small staircase just to the right of them.

He followed her, wondering where she was taking him. During her original tour she showed him this landing. All that was there was a shelf full of stage props and a window. It was an odd bit of design for sure, but not unheard of for tiny nooks like this in older buildings. His curiosity turned to shock as he watched her slide the shelf to the side, revealing a hidden door behind it. Turning the knob, she opened it to reveal a small storage room with a sink, cot, and boxes. It was clear from the messy blanket and open boxes filled with clothes that someone had been living in here.

"I was taking a shower here, because for the past three months I've been living in secret at the theater."

Her softly spoken confession fell in the air around them. Yet another tangle in the web of secrets that had become his life.

Damn.

CHAPTER FOURTEEN

"EXPLAIN."

Piper swallowed hard at Kell's soft demand. She understood his confusion. Most days she was still confused on how she got here. Not the how, really, she knew the exact events that led to her current predicament. But a part of her still couldn't understand how she let them happen.

"I will, but I need a few minutes to..." She waved a hand over her towel-covered form. If she was going to bare the most embarrassing moment of her life, she didn't want to do it while physically bare too. Emotional vulnerability was hard enough. She needed the armor of clothing.

Kell's gaze swept down her body, eyes heating. She clutched the knot on her towel tighter. The temptation to flick it undone and drop the towel overwhelmed her. How she wished she could avoid this conversation by finally giving into the temptation they both so desperately craved.

But she couldn't.

The distraction would only work for a night, and then she'd only be stacking problems on top of each other. Standing her ground, she waited. Kell blinked, the heat in his eyes disappearing. He nodded.

"I'll be right outside."

Once he was outside of the room, door firmly shut, she quickly tossed off her towel. Digging through an open box, she grabbed the first pair of pajamas she saw. The thin cotton shorts and sleep tank covered up barely more than her towel. Like she told Kell earlier, nudity wasn't a huge thing for her that often. Some of her past costumes left hardly anything to the imagination. But for this conversation, around this man, she needed to keep her head clear. With that thought in mind, she grabbed her long fluffy robe from the edge of her bed.

She slipped it on, covering her flower tattoos from sight. Her heart still raced remembering what he'd called her. *A goddess.* That was a comparison she didn't mind. Much nicer than Larry, who told her she reminded him of a tweaked-out cartoon character. Her mood soured at the reminder of who put her in this extremely uncomfortable situation.

"Piper? Are you okay in there?"

Kell's concerned voice simmered her rage, embarrassment flooding back. Her emotions were all over the place. She rubbed her belly. It was giving her a stomachache.

"Yes. You can come in now."

The door creaked open. Kell slowly popped his

head in. He nodded when he saw her fully covered, but she thought she spied a hint of longing still lingering in his gaze.

"What's going on, Piper?" He frowned, crossing his arms over his chest. "Why are you living at the theater?"

Her gaze snagged on his forearms. When in the world had she become so obsessed with forearms? Seriously, they were just another body part. Not even a sexy one. But they were sexy on him. She couldn't drag her attention away from them. She wondered what they would feel like holding her in the dark of night. Her body temperature rose under her robe, sweat gathering on the back of her neck. Or maybe that was a drop of shower water she'd missed.

"Piper?"

"Huh?" What were they talking about? His sexy forearms? No, her squatting here. "Oh, right. Why am I living here. Um…that's a bit of a story."

Kell sat down on her cot, staring up at her with all the patience in the world filling those beautiful blue eyes. "I got nothing but time."

She highly doubted that, but she also sensed he wasn't leaving without an answer. So be it. Taking a deep breath, she started in on her story.

"About a year ago I started dating this guy. Larry."

His eyebrows rose slightly. "Larry? Really? Was he in his fifties?"

She rolled in her lips to stop the giggle from escaping. This was not a moment for laughter. "No, twenty-nine. It was a family name. He was like the fourth-generation Larry or something."

He waved a hand for her to continue.

"Anyway, we met at a bar after one of my shows. Normally I hate bars. They're too crowded and loud. I can never hear what people are saying and there's way too many smells. But I go to celebrate with the cast. I went outside to get a breather, and Larry was there on the back patio. We started talking, he asked for my number and after a few dates we were a couple."

Kell's expression darkened. "Then what?"

If he was surmising this story didn't have her dream happy ending, he was right.

"After a month he wanted to move in together." Fast, she knew, but she'd been in love. Or so she had thought. "We were so great together. No fights, good chemistry. I thought it was the perfect next step in our relationship. I had six months left on my lease, so he just moved in with me."

Kell's jaw tightened. "Please tell me he didn't take over your lease and kick you out."

Worse. Much worse.

"Why, has that happened to you before? I thought you said all of your relationships ended amicably."

"They did." He narrowed his eyes. "Stop deflecting and finish the story."

"Mr. Bossy," she muttered under her breath. The corner of his mouth twitched in a small smile.

"Please continue, Piper."

"Fine," she sighed, hating the next part. "Before I tell you the rest, I want to remind you that I am a self-proclaimed hopeless romantic who believes in true love, and sometimes that can bite me in the butt."

His smile vanished, concern and wariness filling his gaze.

"Larry kept talking about our future, marriage and stuff, and how we should combine our finances."

"Oh no."

Oh yes. Looking back, she realized how naive she'd been, but at the time her eyes had been filled with stars and everything was rose-colored. Her grandparents had gotten married after three weeks of knowing each other. When Larry started talking about happily-ever-after so soon into their relationship, she'd assumed he was just the one. Like Grandpa had been for Grandma.

What was that Kell said earlier about assuming? She'd definitely fit that description when she realized how Larry had tricked her.

"We opened up a joint account. I kept my business account separate." Thank the universe for that small insight. "But all the money for bills, rent and life stuff went into our account. Everything was great for a few months."

He frowned. "What happened after a few months?"

Bile rose up in the back of her throat. She hated this part. Hated admitting how ignorant she'd been. How easily duped. But Kell deserved to know the truth.

"I came home one day, and all his stuff was gone. A lot of my stuff too."

A low growl escaped Kell's throat, but she pressed on.

"I called his cell, but I'd been blocked. Blocked on all his social media too. His friends said they had no clue where he was, and the worst part of it was when I went to check the bank…" Shame filled her as she admitted this next part. "All the money was gone."

Kell let loose a very colorful four-letter curse. Yeah, she'd used that word and several others when she'd found out.

"The bastard stole your money and ran out on you?"

She nodded, humiliation heating her cheeks. She ducked her head, moisture gathering in her eyes. The anger had faded, but she still felt so silly she'd fallen for his love scam. Was she so desperate for someone to love her that she'd believe anyone with sweet words and a nice smile? She was beginning to fear she might never find the love she craved, or perhaps…she simply wasn't worthy of it.

"I didn't have money for the next month's rent. I was evicted after thirty days."

Kell swore again. "And you couldn't find another place?"

She shook her head. "I had no money. Without a security deposit, first and last month's rent, no place would even let me look."

Renting was difficult in normal circumstances—her problem made it impossible. People always thought they were one lotto ticket away from millions, but the truth was most people were one bad day away from losing everything.

"What about staying with friends or family?"

She let out a strangled laugh. "My friends are in the same predicament as me. The Starving Artist is a cliché for a reason. None of them have room for me and I wouldn't burden them like that. As for family...my parents divorced over a decade ago and neither of them has been interested in a relationship with me for longer than that. They never approved of my life choices in anything. We don't really talk anymore."

"They sound like pretty terrible parents," he muttered, eyes filled with anger.

Anger for her? Sweet, but unnecessary. Life was what it was. She learned that a long time ago. It was rarely fair. The only thing one could do was make the best of whatever it handed you.

"My only option was staying here while I saved enough to rent a new place."

One dark eyebrow rose. “Donald lets you stay here?”

Her heart jumped into her throat. Sitting on the cot next to him, she grabbed his hand, staring into his eyes, pleading with everything in her. “No. He has no idea. And you can’t tell him, please. If he knew I was living here it would break the lease, and he’d kick me out. Please, Kell, you can’t tell him. I just need a few more months to get the cash together. Summer camps start next month and they’re always full. I promise I can find a place soon, just please don’t tell anyone.”

Kell stared at her, a thousand thoughts racing across his face, but she couldn’t decipher a single one. She held her breath, waiting, hoping. Finally, he nodded. His hand squeezed hers.

“Of course I won’t tell anyone.” He lifted a hand. “If you stay in my family’s condo.”

“Kell, I can’t—”

“Just until you sort things out,” he insisted. “It’s a short-term rental and we don’t have anyone on the schedule for the next month. We’re redoing the kitchen—some appliances are on back order so it’s out of commission, not rentable. But the rest of the condo is perfect. It’s just sitting empty. You’d be doing me a favor.”

“By squatting?” she asked with a small chuckle.

“No. By keeping an eye on the place while it’s empty and letting me out of the bet so I don’t have to get up in an apparatus.”

"Ha!" She shook a finger at him, recognizing his tactic to sooth her frazzled nerves by teasing her. "Not going to happen, mister. You're getting up in that thing."

He sighed, grasping her hand in his, his face turning serious. "Okay, but please stay in the condo. You can't live here, Piper. It's not safe."

He had a point. The ceiling leaked, and she was risking her lease and her safety staying here all alone with no one knowing. As much as she hated to be a burden to anyone, she could see the worry in Kell's eyes. He didn't make her feel like a burden. He made her feel…safe.

"Okay," she softly agreed.

A relieved breath left him as he smiled.

A weight lifted from her shoulders. Her chest expanded as breath returned. She closed her eyes as a few tears of gratitude leaked out, the warm wetness rolling down her cheeks. Her words were barely a whisper in the small room. "Thank you."

She felt the rough pad of his thumb brush away her tears. Opening her eyes, she stared into the handsome face that haunted her dreams.

"I'm sorry that happened to you." His eyes heated with anger. "If I knew where that bastard was, I'd—"

"Okay, Mr. White Knight, I appreciate the sentiment, but I don't need you to beat up my ex. Karma will get him."

He chuckled. "Of course you would believe in karma. I don't know how you do it."

"Do what?"

"Remain a hopeless romantic after all that."

She shrugged. "I'm not going to let Larry take my money, my home and my sense of wonder. That's too much. I was wrong about him, but that doesn't mean my true love isn't out there waiting for me. Might be silly." She nudged his shoulder with her own, giving him a teasing smile. "But so is believing you're cursed by love."

That got a grin out of him, along with an eye roll. "Touché. And now I'm more motivated than ever to help you fill seats for the show. Why don't you pack up what you need, and we can head over to the condo."

Heart filled with gratitude, she wondered how the universe could put such a wonderful man in front of her, one who was perfect for her in nearly every way and give him the silly notion he was cursed. Maybe she was the key. Maybe she was supposed to show him this curse nonsense wasn't real.

Or maybe she was supposed to break it.

"You really are the sweetest, Kellen."

He smiled, cupping her cheek with his hand and stroking gently. She turned her face into his palm, allowing herself a moment of need.

"Thank you for keeping my secret," she continued. "For not telling Donald. I swear in a month, everything will be okay."

The stroking stopped. He dropped his hand, clearing his throat and staring down at the floor. An odd sense of unease washed over her, but she ignored it. Tonight had been a tidal wave of emotions. They were all crashing in on each other, drowning her in confusion.

"No problem. Donald doesn't have to know anything. I promise."

"Thank you," she said softly, relief filling her. Finally she'd found someone she could trust implicitly.

CHAPTER FIFTEEN

GUILT WAS EATING him alive.

Kell pulled up to the theater, Piper's revelation last night playing over and over in his head. What a grade A jerk her ex was. He wanted nothing more than to find the guy and give him a piece of his mind…among other things. His hand clenched on the steering wheel. He didn't get people like that. How could you pretend to care about someone then up and leave them, taking every penny they had? What kind of monster did that?

Glass houses, my man.

He scowled at his inner voice. It wasn't the same. He wasn't lying to Piper. He was…withholding information he legally couldn't reveal. The rumble in his gut called him a liar. Damn! He had to find a way around that ridiculous contract clause.

At least she had agreed to stay in the condo. Her eyes nearly popped out of her head when she stepped in the two-thousand-square-foot two-bedroom, two-bath home. He hadn't been lying when he said she was doing him a favor. Having someone stay there while they waited to finish the repairs was a huge help. He always hated leaving the rental unoccupied. A sneaky leak could cause thousands in damages. This way, she was helping him while he could help her. It assuaged some of his guilt for the terrible secret he was holding on to. The secret made worse now that he knew she wasn't just losing her studio.

She was losing her home.

No.

Not on his watch.

He had no idea how he was going to help, but determination filled his chest, pushing the guilt down. Even if he had to build Piper a house himself, he'd find a way to make sure she had a place when Donald kicked her out. Hopefully she'd take his help. Unease crawled its way up his spine, tiny pricks of worry poking holes in his plan to save her.

He had to help her. Not just because he felt guilty, but also because he cared for Piper. More than he should. He knew what happened when he fell for someone. The promise to never do it again burned in his soul, but somehow, with each second he spent by her side, Piper was snuffing out that flame. Replacing it with hope for a future.

"Will she even want my help when she finds out?" He spoke the question into the silence of the car.

She might think he was her white knight now,

but when she found out the truth, would he turn into a toad?

He shook his head. He'd been spending too much time in the theater. This job was getting to him if he was sitting here thinking about knights, frogs and fairy-tale solutions to real-world problems. Good thing he planned on outside work today. He needed the space to think.

Grabbing his tool bag, he left his car and headed into the theater. Piper was onstage leading a class of teenagers through a warm-up. Her brown eyes locked with his, excitement and some other emotion he didn't want to name filling them.

"Okay everyone, time for conditioning on the hoops. Five straddle ups, five pullovers, fifteen shoulder shrugs and pull some taffy."

The kids moaned, some of them voicing their distaste for one or more of the exercises she called out. Despite their complaints, he noticed they all raced to grab a hoop. Teenage defiance filled every aspcct of lifc, he guessed.

"Hey," Piper said as he approached the stage.

"Hi. How is the condo?"

She grinned. "Like a dream come true. I swear that bed is made of pure clouds. I've never slept so well in my life."

Her warm smile was infectious, and he couldn't help but smile back.

"What are you working on today?"

He let his gaze drift high. "I'm assessing the

roof today to see what needs to be done. I'm hoping it'll be small fixes I can do on my own, but based on the number of leaks I've found in this place…"

"Ha!" Piper barked out a laugh. "When has any issue here been a small fix?"

"They would have been if Donald would have addressed them earlier." This beautiful historical building was falling apart all because Donald didn't want to spend money making necessary repairs. It made Kell's blood boil.

"Yes, well, as we've determined, Donald is the worst."

He grinned at her wink. On that they could agree.

"Do you need a ladder or anything?" Piper asked, motioning up to the roof.

"No. There's an access point from the attic. Should be good enough to get me up there for an inspection."

A smile curved her beautiful pink lips. "You're willing to climb out a window onto the roof of a building, but you're scared of a little hoop?"

He followed her head as it waved to the stage where the teens were dutifully following her instructions, with a fair bit of complaining and teasing going on too. A shudder racked his body.

"I know how to be safe on a roof. That… I don't know the first thing about that, but it looks painful and dangerous."

A small giggle escaped her. "That's why you learn from a professional, like me. And I wouldn't start you on hoop. Sling is a much more forgiving apparatus. Plus, you lost the taco-truck bet. You have to get up there someday."

"Let's plan on later rather than sooner." He stared at the hoops, grimacing, swearing his body could already feel the pain of falling out of one of those things.

"Kell—"

"Oh, would you look at the time," he interrupted, holding up his wrist, which was free of any watch. Walking backward, he shrugged. "I have to go see a roof about repairs."

Laughter spilled from her lips. She lifted a finger and pointed it at him. "Nice try, mister, but you can't avoid this forever. I will get you up on stage."

He turned, heading toward backstage where the stairs to the attic were. "Can't hear you, too busy working."

Her laughter followed him. Like a balm to his soul. It was the most beautiful laugh he'd ever heard. He swore in that moment to do everything in his power to make sure the tragedy to come didn't destroy that laugh forever. There had to be a way to fix this conundrum he'd gotten himself into. He swore to find it.

He made it onto the roof without issue. The real issue came an hour and a half later after he'd done a thorough inspection and found the results…less than ideal.

"Dammit," he swore, wiping sweat off his brow.

The early summer sun beat down, enhanced by the dark roof shingles. The ones that were still attached. He'd been expecting some work needed, but this…this warranted a call. He slipped back inside the attic and sat on an old wooden stool left up there from some production of past years, no doubt. He pulled out his phone and called Donald. Fifty-fifty on if the guy answered or let it go to voicemail.

"What's the issue now, Thorson?" Donald's angry voice loudly demanded.

Oh yeah, he picked up. Kell sighed, gathering all his customer-pleasing charm he could muster before answering. "Hello, Mr. Noll. I'm calling because I did a full roof inspection today and I'm afraid the results were not what we were hoping for."

A string of four-letter curses pierced his ear. Kell pulled his cell phone away, putting it on speaker. No sense in bursting his eardrum. With the news he had, he was expecting a lot more swearing and shouting.

"From what I can tell, this roof is about twenty years old. That's the general end of lifespan for most roofs. In addition to that, there's significant hail damage from years of storms. Multiple leaks, weather wear and numerous missing shingles. You're going to need an entire roof replacement."

He waited while Donald went through every foul word in the English language and some creative new ones as well. Not shocking. He expected this anger. He also anticipated the next words to come across the line.

"Can we put it on the market without replacing the roof?"

A heavy sigh left him. "We can, but we'll need to take about ten thousand or more off the listing price."

"Ten thousand!" Donald shouted. "What the hell am I paying you for, Thorson? You're supposed to be the best in the business. Fixing and selling, a two-in-one package with the highest sell rate in the state, isn't that what you promised me?"

It was, but he and his brothers also promised to sell high-quality properties. This theater, in its current state even with all the repairs he'd done, was mid-quality at best. The prospective buyers he had would not be happy with the quality. They would demand the price be reduced and Donald would pitch a fit. Better to fix it now and save the headache.

"How much is this repair going to cost me?"

He should quote him an astronomical price, but Kell didn't want to risk Donald pulling the contract and going with another real estate agency. Who would look out for Piper then?

"Shouldn't be too much more." He swallowed down the bile rising in his throat as he tried to assuage this monster of a man. "I can call in my brothers to help. That'll cut down on labor costs and I have an in with a guy who can give me a good deal on premium materials."

"Good," Donald huffed. "But don't worry about premium, go for the cheapest stuff that'll do the job."

"Cheaper material will wear out faster."

"The hell do I care? Leave that problem for the sucker who buys this place."

His grip tightened on the phone as he stared at the screen with Donald's name and the timer of their call ticking away. Five minutes. And every single second felt like an eternity.

"You're the boss," he said through gritted teeth, when what he really wanted to do was reach through the phone and punch the guy. Kell had never been a violent man before, but this slimy jerk was testing his limits.

"Damn right I am, so get on this fast. We only have a few more weeks until the lease is up and I can kick that annoying shrew out and list this place."

Fire burned his chest at Donald's words. A growl rumbled low in his throat. He was two seconds away from telling Donald exactly what he thought when he spoke again.

"She doesn't suspect anything, does she?"

"Pardon?" he asked, clearing his throat when the word came out too rough.

"Pitts. With you there doing all this work, does she see through it? Know I'm gonna sell the place?" There was a slight pause. "You haven't said anything to her, have you?"

"No." The word tore from his throat. "She's just…happy repairs are getting done."

"Good. Keep her in the dark."

He should agree and hang up, but his conscience was so far stretched it felt like one more word could snap it in two.

"Don't you think you should inform your tenant of your decision to sell?"

"Why the hell would I do that?"

Because it was what decent people did. "So she can start looking for a new place. She has to move an entire business. Surely you can see how difficult this will be on her. On her business."

Dark, cruel laughter filled the attic. "I don't give a damn about her business. It's a dog-eat-dog world out there, if she can't handle it, so be it. And don't you dare go spilling the beans to her. We have a contract, Thorson, and if she finds out, I will sue you for every penny you have and destroy your precious little charity along with it."

The man truly was a monster.

"Of course, Mr. Noll. I understand how an NDA works."

"Good. Then get to work on the roof ASAP. Time's wasting."

He was a waste.

Kell stared at his phone as the screen went blank. Taking a few, calming breaths, he fired off an email to his roof-tile guy before texting his brothers the new hitch in this job. Replacing the roof wasn't the problem. They'd done it before. Donald was the real issue. He couldn't wait until they were rid of this client.

But then I'll be rid of Piper too.

The thought struck his chest like a blow. He rubbed at the pain. A throb started behind his left eye. How the hell was he going to fix this situation so nobody got hurt in the end? Was that even possible? He felt like his love curse had spilled over into his work life, determined to doom every aspect of his existence. Nothing he could do about it but press on and hope he found a way to make sure everyone came out on top.

CHAPTER SIXTEEN

PIPER HAD JUST finished rigging the slings for the next class when she spied Kell from the corner of her eye. The teens had all left and sling instruction didn't start for another twenty minutes. Her heart skipped a beat, and she wondered if she could convince Kell to take a small break to chat. She loved talking with him. Odd, since small talk really wasn't her thing. It was uncomfortable and disingenuous. She never understood how neurotypicals navigated such banal chitchat that had no point.

But conversing with Kell was never boring small talk. They talked about real things. He let her gush about her passions, he shared his painful past with her. She still thought the notion of a dating curse was silly, but she was honored he felt comfortable enough with her to be vulnerable and share. They had a real connection, one she cherished and enjoyed.

She was about to open her mouth and suggest a friendly chat when she saw his face. Her mouth hung open, words halted on her tongue.

He looked…angry. She'd never seen Kell angry before. True, she'd barely seen the man outside of the theater, but he'd been frustrated by a few of the repairs over the past three weeks. This, however, didn't look like frustrated anger. His face was pinched, jaw tight, but his eyes were…worried.

She had no idea what put that look on his face, but she made a silent vow to address it right this very minute. Hurrying over to him, she placed a hand on his arm.

"Hey, you okay?"

Kell glanced at her, blinking as his head swiveled, taking in his surroundings. He seemed surprised he was in the theater. What could have him so upset he wandered down from the roof without even realizing it? Now she was really worried.

"Huh? Oh, yeah, yeah. Just…" He scrubbed a hand over his face, letting out a deep sigh. "Work stuff. Nothing you need to worry about."

Normally she'd let that go—she might miss a lot of social cues, but she knew when someone didn't want to talk—but his work stuff currently involved *her* work. "Um, did, uh, you tell Donald about…"

She lifted a hand in the air and waved it toward the small staircase with the prop shelf and her secret room. Her heart pounded in her chest as fear seized her.

She'd been wrong. He was a spy. She let her guard down and he'd told Donald everything. Now she was about to be kicked out and—

Kell snatched her hand out of the air, gripping it between his and holding tightly. His thumbs stroked her skin, warm and rough, but comforting at the same time.

"No. Never. I promised you I wouldn't tell Donald, and I never break a promise, Piper. Never."

She stared into his bright blue eyes. Eyes the color of a summer day. The kind that was filled with hope and promise of good things to come. Closing her eyes, she took a deep breath, her nerves calming at his reassurance. See? She had been right to trust him. Her spy notion was as silly as his curse fears.

"Thank you," she whispered.

One of his hands left hers to cup her cheek. The touch held warmth and reassurance and… something more. Something they both agreed not to explore, but it was getting harder and harder to ignore. Especially when he was being so wonderful. Keeping her secret, providing her with a safe space to live. Not only safe, but fancy too. He cared for her in a way no one else in her life ever had. Giving without expecting anything in return. Tired from fighting this attraction, from hiding her secrets, from the struggles of life in general, she gave in. Piper pressed her face into his palm, seeking the safeguard she felt there. He truly was her knight in shining armor. Or dark flannel technically.

"It's just Donald complaining about the roof and being a giant tool, per usual."

Her eyes popped open, and she grimaced. "Is it that bad?"

He dropped his hands then ran them through his short, dark hair, frustration clear. She missed the contact immediately.

"Yeah. The whole thing needs to be replaced, which he was not happy to hear."

She snorted. "I bet he wasn't."

That got a small smile out of him.

"I managed to convince him a new roof was needed, and my brothers and I can do it at a decent price."

"Your brothers are coming to work on it with you?"

He nodded. "As soon as the materials come in. Should only take us a few days. Week, tops. We'll start the repairs after your show so if any issues occur it won't impact your performances."

She waved a hand in the air. "I'm not worried about that."

He raised one eyebrow. Okay, she'd been a little worried about that. Aerial performances and construction-work sounds did not mesh well.

"I'm sorry Donald was being such a jerk," she said.

"It is what it is. At least he agreed to the repair or…things might get dicey during hail season."

He paused before he said the last part, as if it

wasn't what he originally intended to say. She noticed he did that sometimes. Like he was going to say one thing, thought better of it and said something else. She had no idea what that was about, but considering she wasn't the most skilled at conversation either, she let it go.

His shoulders were still tight, body tense. A call with Donald would do that to anyone. An idea sparked in her mind. Good thing she knew exactly how to ease the tension a rage-inducing conversation with her scummy landlord caused.

"Come with me." She grabbed his hand and tugged him onto the stage.

"Wait, Piper, what are—"

"Just come," she insisted, pulling him to center stage where she'd hung her favorite purple sling.

"Oh no. Hell no." Kell shook his head, dropping her hand and crossing his arm over his chest. "You are not getting me up in that death trap."

She couldn't contain the eye roll. "You spent all morning up on a roof that's falling apart. If anything is a death trap, I wouldn't say it's my job."

He frowned, shaking his head. "No."

Sticking out her bottom lip, she gave him her best sad eyes. "Please? I swear there's nothing better to relieve tension than spinning in a sling."

His frown turned into a devilish grin, gaze sweeping over her with heat as he cocked one eyebrow. "Nothing? Cause I can think of something much more...horizontal."

She swallowed, her throat drier than it had ever been before. Other parts of her were so hot and damp she felt as though she'd just done an hour-long spin tolerance class. How could this man turn her on with nothing but a look and a bit of innuendo?

"Mind out of the gutter, mister. I have a class in twenty minutes."

He chuckled, and a rush of butterflies took flight in her stomach.

"Besides, you have to get in the sling. You lost the bet, remember?"

He groaned. "Okay, you win. What do I do?"

Yes! She loved winning. Loved teaching aerials even more. And she especially loved introducing the art to people who would never think to try it in a million years. Kell fit that description to a T.

"It would be better if you were wearing different clothes." She frowned as she took in his appearance.

Kell glanced down at his jeans and dark blue flannel. "We should probably wait until I can find some spandex or something, right?"

"Nice try, buddy." Now all she could think about was Kell in spandex. "But you're not weaseling out of this. I did an entire routine in jeans and a leather corset once. It sucked, but I made it work and so can you. Though you should take the flannel and your shoes off."

His fingers worked the buttons, deftly flicking

them open one by one. He shrugged the overshirt off his shoulders, revealing a tight-fitting black T-shirt underneath. He placed his flannel on the stage floor, his biceps flexing with the movement. A wave of heat scorched her skin as sweat gathered on the back of her neck. She wished she could blame it on the broken AC, but that had been one of the first things Kell had repaired. No, this heat wave was all due to the man in front of her. Ridiculous. She'd seen dozens of fit people in her years as an aerialist. Kell's arms were no different than anyone else's.

Except they were.

Because they were his.

"Now what?" he asked after he'd taken his shoes off.

She shook off the naughty thoughts playing in her mind and focused on the task at hand.

"First I'm going to have you stand with the sling around your back and in your armpits."

He frowned. "I don't follow."

She guided him to the fabric, positioning him where she wanted him. "Now grab the fabric with your hands and we're going to try an invert."

"A what?"

"Invert. Put the fabric on your lower back and bring your knees up to the outside of the fabric and lean back."

He raised one eyebrow in disbelief.

"Trust me, you can do this."

Shaking his head he followed her instruction. The sling was low enough that with some help from her he managed to invert without too much trouble.

"Good. Now I'm going to give you a little spin." She pushed on one of his knees, giving him a slow spin.

"I feel ridiculous," he said.

She held back a snort of laughter. He did look a bit silly. "You look great. Like Spider-Man."

He chuckled. "Liar."

"No, really. I call this pose Spider-Man for my kids' class. Upside down with your knees bent, you totally look like the friendly neighborhood superhero."

Kell let go of the fabric with his right hand, moving it in front of him to do the classic Spider-Man web-shooting pose. Unfortunately, as a newbie with no sense of balance yet, releasing the fabric caused his body weight to shift in the sling. He started to pitch to one side. Thankfully his knees were still on the outside of the fabric, keeping him in the sling even as he slid to one side, landing in a front balance.

"Oof, damn!" Kell dropped his other hand, losing all connection with the sling and sliding out onto the mat, landing on his backside.

"Kell! Are you okay?" She rushed to his side, sitting on the mat beside him, grateful to see a smile on his face as he looked up at her.

"That was…something. Glad I tried it. Bet fulfilled." He winked.

Playfully smacking his shoulder, she pointed a finger at him. "Oh, come on, that was barely one move and you were doing great until you let go."

"You never seem to hold on when you're practicing."

He watched her practice? Of course he saw her practice, the man was here every day working. Logically he would catch a glimpse or two of her during that time. It didn't mean anything that he watched her. Only…it did. It meant a lot to her.

"I have years of study and practice," she responded. "You are a novice, so hands on the fabric until you're comfortable enough to let go."

"Honestly, I'd rather watch you. You're beautiful in the air, Piper. Like a fairy, soaring through the sky. Your face lights up, radiating joy. Anyone who watches you can tell this is your calling."

All the air left her lungs—no, left her entire body. Stunned, she stared. What response could she give to that? How did this man render her speechless with such beautiful words? Words that burrowed their way into her soul and lit up every inch of her being.

"Thank you," she finally mumbled. Because that's what you were supposed to do when someone complimented you, right? Thank them. What he said was so far beyond a compliment her gratitude felt paltry.

"It's the truth." He nodded, lifting a hand to brush a strand of hair behind her ear.

Her body trembled at his touch. She was so tired of holding back, so tired of denying herself the one thing she wanted. Maybe that's why she opened her mouth, and words fell out without thought or reason.

"Kell, do you ever think it's not a curse, but you just keep meeting the wrong people?"

His fingers lingered on her cheek, eyes gazing deeply into hers. "I don't know. You're the one who believes in happily-ever-after and fairy tales. By your logic, maybe it is a curse and the only thing that can break it is true love's kiss."

Normally a line like that would have her groaning and running for the hills, but she heard the yearning behind his words. Kell wanted to believe, even if he professed the opposite. She could do that for him. She could prove to him that love, real love, was out there for everyone, including him.

Leaning forward, she placed her palms on his shoulders, then slid her hand around the back of his neck as she tilted her head. His palm cupped her cheek as he drew her to him, dipping his head. He hesitated, allowing her to have the final say in what was clearly a line they were about to cross.

She'd been doing aerials for over a decade. Dropped from heights of over twenty feet, even done a silks photo shoot hanging off the bottom of a hot-air balloon. None of those experiences were as terrifying as this moment. Because she knew, deep in her soul, the second their lips touched, her life would never be the same.

Eyelids drifting shut, she closed the distance between them. The second her lips brushed his, fireworks exploded behind her closed eyes. A rush, unlike anything she got from doing a drop, plunged her heart down to her toes and back up again. Her skin prickled with electricity. His hand moved to the back of her neck, gripping tighter, pressing her closer as he swept his tongue out, seeking entrance. She gladly complied, reveling in the taste of this man who had tempted her for far too long.

Her heart cheered in triumph even as her brain shouted out a small protest. Whatever. She'd deal with the consequences of her rash actions later. Right now, she was drowning in a sea of blissful sensation. Good heavens, Kell could kiss! Her body demanded more. Just as she was about to debate breaking her rule of no hookups, the sound of laughter pierced the air.

Kell pulled away just as the theater doors slammed open, revealing a group of students here for the sling class. Breathing heavily, Piper touched her fingers to her lips, the feel of Kell still there. She feared it always would be. A brand on her soul.

His bright blue eyes, filled with heat, stared at her with longing. "I'm sorry."

"I'm not." The words were out before she could

stop them. Not that she intended to. She wasn't sorry for what happened, and she didn't want him to be either. "I enjoyed kissing you."

A slow grin spread across his face. "Me too."

Relief filled her at his words.

"I should get back to work." He nodded to the students coming in. "You too, it seems."

He stood, helping her up which was nice since her legs had turned to jelly the moment their mouths met. Squeezing her hand, he turned, grabbed his discarded things and headed backstage. She watched him go, doing her best to hold on to the warm feeling in her chest and ignore the sharp warning in her gut that everything was about to change.

CHAPTER SEVENTEEN

FIVE DAYS.

It had been five very long days since he'd lost his head and kissed Piper. Technically she kissed him, but he kissed her back. Even though he knew it had been a bad idea, he couldn't find it in himself to regret it. Even now, nearly a week later, he could still taste her sweetness on his lips. Still feel the warmth of her body heating his. Every fiber of his being wanted a repeat performance.

But work had gotten hectic the past few days with prepping everything for the roof repair, and Piper had been consumed with tech and dress rehearsal for her show. Other than a few friendly waves, rushed hellos and adorable pink blushes as she spied him across the theater, they hadn't had a chance to speak.

All that ended tonight.

He had to talk to her. Make sure she was okay and see what she wanted to do about this line they stepped over. Forget it happened? He hoped not. He knew what he wanted to do, but he also knew if they started anything it would be temporary.

That's all he could offer her. Since she'd made her stance on casual very clear, he didn't see how they could pursue anything without one of them getting hurt in the end.

He was usually the man with the plan, but right now he was lost. Logic told him to forget it. Move on. They were too different, wanted the complete opposite things, not to mention the curse still looming over his head. But he'd be damned if he made a decision without asking Piper first. One lesson his mother drilled into his head growing up was to respect people's decisions and not make choices for them. He'd talk to Piper. After the show, of course. No need to add more nerves to her night.

Gripping the bouquet of roses, he adjusted his tie and slipped backstage. The theater was already half full and people were still pouring in. He blinked, eyes adjusting to the dim light backstage as performers hurried around him frantically.

"Kell? What are you doing back here?"

He turned at the voice that made his heart skip a beat. The air left his lungs as he saw Piper. She wore all black, her hair pulled back into a ponytail, a clipboard in hand. She was beautiful, even as she blended into the shadows.

Lifting the bouquet, he started to answer her. "I came to wish you good lu—"

Her eyes widened, and she squashed her hand over his mouth, halting his words. "Don't say it!"

"Say what?" he tried to ask, but the words came out muffled behind her hand.

"The G L phrase. It's bad luck to say that in the theater. I thought your mom was some fancy cultural arts person."

His eyes shifted down to her hand, eyebrows rising. Huffing, she dropped her hand, glare still directed at him. He ducked his head to hide his smile.

"You're right. I should have known better, but 'break a leg' sounds wrong to say to an aerialist before a performance."

"We don't say that either."

"Then what do you say for lu—well wishes," he corrected himself at her warning glare.

"We're dancers, we say merde. It's French for..." She glanced behind her to where couple of kids stood a few feet away, hopping up and down with preshow excitement. "Well, it's just what we say."

He knew a little French, which was why he understood her hesitation to translate the swear in earshot of kids. What he didn't know was why that word was considered good luck for dancers.

"Of course, well then." Lifting the flowers, he bowed slightly. "Merde."

Her scowl eased into a smile as she took the bouquet from his hands, bringing them to her face and inhaling. "Thank you. These are beautiful. You didn't have to."

"I know." He gazed into those beautiful brown

eyes, so dark and warm he wanted to sink into them. "I wanted to."

A pink blush rose on her cheeks. "You look very handsome tonight."

He felt his own cheeks warm at her praise. "Thank you, and you look beautiful as always, but I'm confused on the costume. Isn't this *Romeo and Juliet*?"

He knew they couldn't perform in traditional Shakespearean costumes while doing aerials, but why was she wearing all black?

"Oh, I'm not performing. I'm the director and one of the riggers. Gotta stay out of sight." She waved a hand at her dark clothing.

"Ah, that makes sense." A small part of him lamented the fact that he wouldn't get to see her perform tonight. The few times he'd seen her in the air had been entrancing. While he was sure her students would be amazing, Piper's entire soul lit up with joy when she was in the air. It was awe-inspiring to see. "Well, I should find my seat. It's filling up out there."

"I wanted to ask you about that." She stared up at him with wonder. "We sold out both performances. We've never done that before. How did you do that?"

"You assume it was me? Maybe word got out about how amazing you and your students are."

She arched one dark eyebrow. A chuckle left him.

"Okay," he admitted. "I did tell you I was going

to do my best to help, but I can't take all the credit. I contacted my mother. She put out the word to her friends. Patrons of the arts, if you will. They jumped at the chance to see such a unique performance of a classic. She sends her regrets on being unable to attend. She's in London right now."

Piper clutched the roses to her chest. "Please give her my sincere thanks."

He nodded. "I will."

As he started to turn to head to his seat, the soft feel of her hand on his arm stopped him.

"Kell?"

"Yeah?"

A hint of worry filled her eyes. He hated it. Wanted to erase the emotion from her entire world.

"Could, um, could we talk after the show?"

Since that was his plan exactly, he nodded. "Of course."

"Good, good." She shifted on her feet, something else clearly on her mind. "There's another ritual in the theater for a good show that some people participate in."

"Really?" While his mother was on the cultural arts board and he attended many plays, he rarely saw the inner workings of the theater. "What is it?"

She looked up at him through her lashes, a faint blush on her cheeks as she whispered, "A kiss for luck."

He roared inside, holding his body very still when what he really wanted to do was take her in his arms and devour her. It had to be a good sign that she wanted another kiss, right? Clearly she wasn't angry with him for the previous one if she wanted a repeat performance. Perhaps their talk later would go the way he hoped.

Cupping her face, he leaned down and softly brushed his lips across hers once. Twice. The barest of tastes, tormenting them both, but he didn't want to push. This was her choice. Her decision. A moment later, Piper rose on her toes, pressing her mouth firmly against his, opening slightly. He took her hint, deepening the kiss. She tasted like sunshine and hope.

Far too soon for his liking, Piper pulled back. They were both breathing heavily, but the smile on her face made his chest swell.

"I'll see you after the show," he whispered.

She nodded. Someone called her name, and she turned, running off to put out whatever preshow emergency had come up. Slipping out from backstage, he moved to the audience, glancing at the room, now nearly full, for an empty seat. His eyes spotted an empty chair in the middle of the front row with a sign on it. A small chuckle left him as he realized it said Reserved For and his name on it.

He sat, recognizing several people in the audience from his family's circles. Mom had called in all the bigwigs. He'd have to give her something extra special this Mother's Day. The lights overhead dimmed as the preshow music started. The din of the audience hushed, the curtain opened. Showtime.

Kell sat, watching the show in amazement. The performers on stage did a fantastic job of depicting *Romeo and Juliet* with no dialogue. Even if he didn't know the play by heart, he would still be able to follow the story. Their movements were infused with emotion and the music matched the energy.

He was so proud of Piper. What she created here was amazing. Not just the show, but everything with this theater. The grim reminder of what was about to happen to it, to her, stabbed him in the gut. He had to find a way to save the theater, for her. He could not let the end of this job be a tale of woe.

CHAPTER EIGHTEEN

NOTHING SOUNDED BETTER than the cheers of a wowed audience. Nothing except Kell in his rich, deep voice telling her she was beautiful. Her heart fluttered as the performers took their final bow. What a night it had been. Opening night was always stressful, but the cast rocked it. No one fell from an apparatus, a cue wasn't missed and they had a full house giving a standing ovation. All thanks to her students' hard work and the promise of a sweet, sexy contractor who stood front-row center, cheering louder than anyone.

"Damn you, Kell," she whispered, hiding in the shadows backstage. Why was he so wonderful? It was impossible to resist him. She knew starting anything with him would be a bad idea. As long as he held fast to his silly curse notion it would only end in heartbreak. Her heartbreak.

But what if I can be the one to break the curse?

She didn't actually believe he was cursed. She might be a hopeless romantic, but she was still grounded in reality. All he needed was someone to prove to him that he wasn't a stepping stone to a better partner. That was easy. She doubted there was a better man in all the world.

The only reason it hadn't worked with any of his exes was because they weren't the one for him. Was she? Who could say, but she knew one thing deep in her soul. If she let Kell get away without even trying to see if there was something real there, she'd regret it for the rest of her life. This wasn't like her previous relationships. She wasn't letting her romantic notions sweep her away. She'd been fighting this thing for Kell since the beginning. It was different this time. Maybe that meant it was right. Maybe Kell was the one she'd been waiting for all along. Which was why she asked to talk to him after the show, and why the butterflies in her stomach were currently fluttering into a tornado of nerves.

The houselights came back up as the performers hurried backstage. She called out "Good show" to them as they rushed past her.

"Remember, we have another show tomorrow night so get lots of rest."

They normally had weeklong runs, but since this was a student performance there were only two shows. Two sold-out shows. She still couldn't believe Kell had managed to do that. No way could a man that sweet be cursed. The universe would never.

The audience filed out. All except one person.

Rachel's voice sounded from behind her. "Hottie handyman sure looks good in a suit."

Piper let out a startled squeak, dropping the curtain she'd been hiding behind as she stared at Kell. He did look unfairly handsome in his dark charcoal three-piece suit. She'd never been one for suits on men—they always looked better on women, in her opinion—but Kell in a suit made her forget there were still people in the building. Scratch that, the world.

"Don't sneak up on me like that," she scolded.

Rachel snorted. "I wasn't sneaking. You were too busy drooling at the guy you like to notice the fact that everyone has left except him and me."

She blinked, glancing around the dimly lit backstage. Silence filled the air. Rachel was right. Everyone was gone. Not surprising. They had another show, so it wasn't like anyone needed to stay to help derig, but normally she noticed as people left and called goodbye.

"Oh no." Worry crept up her neck. "I hope I wasn't rude by not saying goodbye to anyone."

She was usually very diligent about her goodbyes after a show, reminding her cast what an amazing job they did.

"Don't worry about it." Rachel waved a hand in the air. "Everyone was riding the high of a full house. It's understandable that your attention would be focused on the man who made that happen. Seriously, how did he do that?"

When she found out they'd sold every seat in the house, she'd admitted to Rachel that Kell had helped with ticket sales. Her bestie had suggested hiring him on as their marketing manager. Ha! Like she would ever have the funds to hire a marketing person.

"His mother is on an art council," she answered. "I guess she made some calls to patrons of the arts."

"Wow. Sweet, handy and has a good relationship with his mother." Rachel arched her neck, a smile curling her dark red lips. "And he cleans too."

Whipping her head around she stared out in the audience where Kell was going row by row, picking up discarded programs. Her heart flipped. That did it. She couldn't resist this man any longer. No matter what he thought about love and curses, she had to try.

"Piper." Rachel's voice held a hint of caution. "I know that look."

"What look?" she asked, focus still zeroed in on Kell.

"The one where your eyes turn into hearts like some kids' cartoon."

"That's not physically possible."

"You know what I mean," Rachel insisted. "I know I've been singing Kell's praise here, but remember the guy is antilove."

She blinked, turning her gaze back to her friend. "I know, but that's only because he thinks he's cursed. Don't people who believe in curses also believe they can be broken?"

"Oh, babe."

"No, I'm serious. Besides, you were the one who said I should loosen up. Go with the flow more."

Rachel's teeth came out to worry her bottom lip as concern filled her face. "I know, but I mean have a one-night stand with a stranger. Not hook up with a guy who is antidating. I know you, Piper. I don't want you getting your heart broken. Again."

"I won't." She whispered the words, feeling the truth of them fill her. She knew starting anything with Kell would be a risk, but she had to take it. She'd hate herself forever if she missed out on what could be the love of her life.

"If he hurts you, I'm gonna kill him."

She laughed softly. "No, you won't. Naya would be so mad if you went to jail for murder."

"Ha! She'd help me cover it up."

Rachel's girlfriend, Naya, was a sweetheart who Piper adored. She doubted the kind woman would hurt a fly, although she was extremely protective of her girlfriend, so who knew.

"We haven't even started anything yet." They might not start anything. As of now, this was all speculation. "Save the threats for possible future times. And get out of here. I'm sure Naya is out front with the car waiting for you."

Rachel sighed, pulling her in for a fierce hug. "Fine. But please, just remember to take care of your heart first. Make that man show you a good time, but don't fall unless he's falling too."

"You worry too much."

"I'm your best friend. It's my job."

She squeezed Rachel tight, grateful to have someone in her life she knew she could always count on. They might not have worked out as a couple, but she was so glad life kept them connected. As she pulled away, her gaze went back to Kell. What she felt for him was decidedly not friendly. It was…more, and even if it blew up in her face and ripped her heart out, she knew she had to give it a go or she'd never be able to sleep at night for the what ifs.

Rachel left, waving goodbye to Kell on her way. Then the theater was empty, except for them.

"You don't have to do that," she said, coming out to center stage and sitting on the edge.

Kell glanced over at her with a smile. He made his way to where she sat, stack of paper programs in hand. Placing them on the stage next to her, he stood in front of her with a smile. The edge she sat on made her the perfect height to stare into his beautiful blue eyes.

"I know, but I feel a little bad that so many people left their programs in their seats. Whatever happened to theater decorum?"

She laughed. "Aerial shows tend to be a little rowdier than stage plays."

"I did notice a lot of cheering and wooing during the performance. Can't say I blame anyone. It was amazing. A few of those drops had me gripping my seat in terror, I'll admit. How do you all do that without screaming?"

"The terror is half the fun." She winked.

Kell threw back his head and laughed. The sound wrapped around her like a warm blanket, filling her with the courage to open her mouth and say what was on her mind.

"About the other day..." Her heart started to race as nerves set in.

His laughter died, gaze coming back to hers, a pensive expression filling his face.

"You know the day we..." She waved a hand to the spot on the stage where they'd shared a kiss. Kell arched one eyebrow, remaining silent. "When *I* kissed you."

The corner of his lips quirked up. "I believe I remember that."

She swatted at him playfully. With a chuckle, he grabbed her hand, then stroked her palm with his thumb, eyes going serious.

"I also remember kissing you back and enjoying it immensely."

The racing eased at his confession. She'd assumed from his enthusiastic participation—and their preshow kiss earlier—he'd been as into it as her, but decoding people's feelings had never been her strong suit. Her autistic need for directness had been a problem in past relationship. She appreciated Kell not expecting her to infer.

"Me too." She smiled. "Enjoyed it, I mean."

He took a step closer, fitting himself between her legs as she sat on the edge of the stage floor, legs dangling off the end. He placed his hands on either side of her hips, leaning down until she could feel the warmth of his breath blow across her cheek as he whispered in her ear.

"Can I confess that I want to do it again?"

She rolled her lips in to keep from squealing like a schoolgirl. Instead, she lifted her hands, placing them on his shoulders.

"I'd like that."

His lips kissed her jaw, just below her ear. The barest of touches that sent a shock wave of heat straight to all her good parts. A small moan escaped her lips as his mouth traveled down her cheek with slow, torturous movements. Unable to fight it any longer, she turned her head, capturing his lips with her own. A growl left his throat, vibrating against her mouth. She let out a surprised squeak as his hand gripped her hips, pulling her closer to the edge of the stage until she was flush against his body.

Colors exploded behind her closed eyelids. All thought left her brain as pure rapture filled her every waking thought. She couldn't speak, couldn't think. All she could do was feel. And all she could feel was the fire this man was stoking inside her.

She nearly lost her head and pulled him on stage to have her wicked way with him, but a tiny voice inside reminded her that they needed to talk first.

"Wait," she panted, pushing on his shoulder lightly as she pulled her lips from his.

Kell moved back, breathing heavily. Concern marred his brow. "What's wrong?"

"We need to talk first."

Realization dawned on his face. He blinked, as if only now seeing where he was and what they were doing. A flicker of something flashed in his eyes… Was that shame? Why was he ashamed?

"I'm sorry," he said, stepping back. "I didn't mean to—"

"Stop." She held up a hand. "Before you say anything else I might misinterpret, I need to say something."

He nodded, mouth shut tight.

"I like you, Kell." There, she said it. As scary as it was to think it, saying it out loud had been surprisingly easy. She felt lighter now, freer. "I enjoy spending time with you, and I'd like to do it more. Outside of, you know, here and emergency room visits."

He chuckled, smiling. "Don't forget delicious taco trucks and seafood restaurants."

"Those too," she said with a smile. "I was thinking we could hang out, maybe catch a movie or something? As more than…friends."

His smile slipped. "You mean…like dates?"

Fear started to claw its way up her throat. She nodded, rushing to explain. "I know how you feel about dating and you know how I feel."

"Completely opposite, you mean?" he said with a sad smile.

"Exactly, but maybe we can meet in the middle somewhere."

He frowned. "How do you mean?"

"I know you think you're cursed," she said, reaching out and grabbing his hand in hers. "But curses can be broken. You said it yourself—true love's kiss. Why not give this thing between us a shot? If it works out, amazing."

"And if it doesn't?" he said softly.

A heavy pain filled her, but she knew if she didn't at least give this a try, she'd regret it forever. "Then we go our separate ways."

He stared at their joined hands, squeezing gently as his gaze found hers again. A wealth of pain, fear and hope burned from their blue depths. She held on to that last emotion with everything inside her.

"I don't want to hurt you," he confessed softly.

"Then don't." She tugged gently and he stepped closer. "Just be honest with me, no matter what you're feeling. Tell me if you're scared or angry or bored. Maybe we try this thing and it's not a fit, I'm not the one to break your curse."

He looked up at her with an indulgent smile. "Really going all in on the fairy-tale stuff, huh?"

"Shh."

He mimed zipping his lips and she had to hold in a laugh.

"All I'm saying is there's something here between us, we both know that. If we don't try to see what it is, where it could lead, we could regret it for the rest of our lives. I know I would."

He nodded. "Me too."

The weight of anxiety on her chest lifted, joy filling her as he released her hand and cupped her face in his warm palms.

"Okay," he said softly. "Let's give this thing a try."

Joy erupted inside her. Piper couldn't believe this was happening. She knew this could be a colossal mistake. Kell still thought he was cursed, but he was giving this a shot. Giving *them* a shot. One wrong move and he'd put that wall up around his heart again.

I won't let that happen. I'll show him just how loveable he is.

Because the truth was, she cared for him. Deeper than even she ever thought she could care for another person. Kell was sweet, kind and deserved all the love and happiness in the world. She was determined to show him that tonight. Now that they'd agreed to see each other, she couldn't wait another second to have him.

"Come here," she said with a beckoning finger. "I want you to see something."

She stood, moving across the stage to where

a lone mat was set up from the ending act. The soft sound of Kell's footsteps followed her as he climbed onto the stage, stopping right beside her.

"What is it?"

"Down here."

She lay down on the mat and patted the space beside her. He followed, their shoulders pressing together, her heart racing at the contact.

"Look," she said, pointing up.

"Wow." Kell's soft exclamation sounded in the air.

The stage lights were off, but the houselights from the audience cast a glow on the slings and hoops hung high in the rafters. The reflections off the metal rigging bits caused sparkles of light to shoot through the air like twinkling stars in the night sky.

"It's magical," he said, voice filled with awe. His gaze turned to her, heat burning in those bright blue eyes. "Just like you."

She couldn't stop the smile from curling her lips. Sliding a hand around the back of his neck, she tugged, pulling him to her. He went willingly, latching his mouth on to hers in a soul-consuming kiss. He pressed the full length of his body against hers, but it still wasn't enough to quell the fire burning her from the inside out. She arched up, fusing their bodies together through the fabric they both wore. It wasn't close enough.

Dropping her hands, she quickly started to tug at his clothing. Kell chuckled above her.

"Eager?"

"You have no idea. Lose the clothes, mister," she demanded.

He stood. She lamented the loss of his warmth for two seconds before he quickly stripped his clothing off and her jaw dropped wide. Hello, Hottie Handyman! It was clear Kell's job in construction paid off. His body was a work of art that would make a sculptor weep. She wanted to touch every inch of skin she could see…and she could see all of it.

"Your turn," his deep voice commanded.

A command she was only happy to oblige. Sitting up, Piper made quick work of her shirt and pants. Tossing them off to who-cared-where and leaving her in nothing but her new black bra and panty set. Had she specifically bought it with Kell in mind? Yes. Had it been smart to spend money on frivolous lingerie when she had other bills to worry about? No. Was the hungry look in Kell's eyes worth it? Absolutely yes!

"You are the most beautiful goddess I have ever seen," he growled, climbing back on the mat and coming over to her.

She giggled, the sound turning into a moan when he latched his mouth onto that sweet spot on her neck just below her ear. His hands caressed her bare skin, fingers making quick work of divesting her of her undergarments.

"Shoot, hold on," he said, moving to his discarded clothing and pulling his wallet from his pants pocket. He pulled out a foil packet, quickly tearing it open and protecting them both. Good thing he'd been prepared because she was so far gone, she could barely remember her name, let alone being safe. She hadn't exactly planned for this to happen.

But she was so glad it was happening.

He placed himself at her entrance, pausing as he stared into her eyes. She gasped at the emotions she saw swimming in their clear blue depths.

"Piper," he said softly. "I want you to know how much you mean to me. This is… You are special."

Tears blurring her vision, she blinked them away, swallowing past the emotion clogging her throat she replied. "You're special too, Kell."

His mouth fused to hers as he joined them together. Universes exploded and formed behind her eyes at the feel of their connection. A rush, bigger than any aerial drop she'd ever performed, sent her heart racing through the stratosphere. They moved in unison, as if they'd done this dance for lifetimes. As she felt the wave of completion wash over her, Kell quickened his pace, joining her in the bliss that was their souls and bodies becoming one.

Piper melted inside. Hope filled her even as that tiny voice warned this could all end in disaster. She ignored the voice, staring at the twinkling lights above, seeing only their beauty and the beauty of this moment. Gloom and doom had no place in the start of what she hoped would be her very own happily-ever-after.

CHAPTER NINETEEN

"WHEN WAS THE last time this roof was repaired, Kell?" Cash grabbed a roof shingle, which proceeded to crumble like a dried leaf in his hand.

Kell let out a heavy sigh, anger rising in his gut again at Donald's shoddy landlord duties. "As far as I can tell, Mr. Noll hasn't done any significant repairs to the place since he purchased it fifteen years ago."

"What the hell?" Cash tossed the remaining chunk of shingle off the roof. It sailed through the air, landing in the large dumpster they'd rented below. "No wonder this roof is a mess. I'm surprised the whole theater isn't flooded."

"There are a lotta leaks due to the roof, but thankfully no major damage. Took a lot to convince Donald to even address the roof."

"Sounds like a real jerk," Mal grunted, ripping up shingles and tossing them down.

His brother didn't know the half of it. Donald was a real piece of work. He'd be glad when this job was done.

"Hello up there," a melodic voice called from the attic window.

Kell glanced up to see Piper sticking her head out, a bright smile on her face. His heart skipped a beat, reminding him a part of him very much wasn't looking forward to the end of this project. What was he going to do about Piper? Things had gotten doubly complicated since their magical night after her first show.

He'd gone out with the cast after their final show and enjoyed seeing Piper receive the praise of the cast. The bar had been noisy and crowded, not an issue for him, but she'd clearly felt overwhelmed after a bit. He offered to leave with her, but she didn't want to disappoint everyone, so they wandered out to the back patio, which was quieter and less congested. They spent the night chatting about favorite movies and books. She, of course, loved everything romance while he preferred documentaries and mysteries. It had been a wonderful night that ended with him taking her back to the condo and making out in his car for hours before moving their activities to his back seat, which was not as spacious as he'd like, but they'd been so far gone they couldn't wait.

He hadn't done that since he was a teenager.

But now he had significant heartburn eating away at him. The guilt of the secret he held was manifesting into physical ailments. He had to find a way to tell her Donald was selling the place without violating his contract and risking his charity. But how?

"I got y'all some ice-cold root beer." Piper climbed out onto the roof, three bottles in hand, the necks between her fingers.

His heart jumped into his throat. As carefully as possible, he hurried over to her.

"Hey, don't come out here. It's dangerous."

She gazed up at him with an indulgent smile. "Seriously? You know what I do for a living. Standing on a perfectly solid roof is much safer than doing an ankle hang fifteen feet in the air."

He wasn't entirely sure what an ankle hang was, but based on the name, he bet he didn't want to know. Especially if she was the one demonstrating it. He knew she was trained, but one of these days she was going to give him a heart attack with those tricks.

"Different kind of danger," he insisted. "Besides, there's rules about who can be on a roof when we're fixing it, safety and legal stuff."

"Shoot, I'm sorry." She quickly scrambled back inside the attic window, popping her head out again and holding the bottles aloft. "I just didn't want you guys getting dehydrated up here."

Her kindness warmed his heart, easing the racing panic that started the second he saw her climb onto the roof. Reaching out, he took the bottles from her grasp with one hand and cupped her cheek with the other. Placing a soft kiss to her lips, he rubbed his nose against hers.

"And that is why you are the sweetest person to ever exist."

She giggled. "If bringing you cold drinks while you work on a hot day makes me the sweetest, you, sir, have a very low bar."

She had no idea. The people in his world operated on a "you scratch my back, and I'll scratch yours" policy. No one did anything simply because they were trying to help others. It was all about how you could benefit, get richer, look better. Even Donald was trying to spend as little as possible to fix this place just to turn it around and sell it at the highest profit he could weasel.

And I'm helping him do it.

Bile rose in his gut at the reminder.

"You must be the famous Piper," Cash said, carefully making his way toward them.

"I'm famous?" She gave Kell a cheeky look.

"Kell says you dance like an 'angel in the sky,' and that's a direct quote."

"Oh, really?"

Cash nodded. "Yup, you've got Old Kell here starstruck. I swear you're all he talks about these days. 'Piper is amazing. She's so sweet and beautiful and you should see her drop from the ceiling. It takes ten years off my life, but it's amazing.' He can't stop talking about you. Like a lovesick schoolgirl."

"Enough, Cash." Kell sighed. *Someone save him from annoying little brothers.* "And what's with the 'old' stuff? You're only two years younger than me, punk. Piper, I'm sorry for him. This is my brother Cash, who doesn't know when to shut up."

"That's me," Cash said with a grin.

"And that's Mal." He pointed to Mal who was focused on the task of ripping up the old shingles but offered a small wave in their direction.

"Nice to meet you both," Piper said, her smile warm and inviting. "I don't mean to interrupt your work, I just wanted to make sure you don't melt out here."

It was a warm summer day, but thankfully they had some cloud cover blocking the sun from blazing down on them. He passed two of the cold drinks to Cash, bending down to place another quick kiss to her addictive lips.

"See that right there? The sweetest."

She blushed, the pink hue flushing across her cheeks in stark contrast to the dark blue streaks in her hair.

"I have a class in a few minutes, but don't hesitate to reach out if you need anything. Nice to meet you, Cash. Mal."

Cash popped the top of his root beer, lifting it in a toast to her. "Likewise, angel."

He glowered at his brother. The man couldn't stop flirting to save his life. Cash just grinned, giving him a wink as he took a deep sip of his drink. Mal grunted, offering a half wave as Piper ducked back into the attic and disappeared into the building.

Once she was gone, he turned to find both of his brothers frowning at him. With Mal that was par for the course. He didn't think he'd ever seen his grumpy baby brother smile. But Cash? Cash was never without a grin, smart-alecky or genuine.

"What?" he asked, twisting the top off his own drink and tossing it down to the dumpster.

"She's nice. I like her."

"I do too." What was Cash so upset about?

"Have you told her about Donald's plans to sell yet?"

He glanced back to the window, worried she might have overhead. Or hopeful she had? If she overheard about Donald's plans to sell, it wouldn't be his fault, right? That wasn't breaking the contract. Damn, he was grasping at straws trying to solve this problem. And it wouldn't work anyhow. If she discovered the sale from him in any way, he could be held liable, and Donald could sue. Even if it was an accident.

"No. You know I can't tell her."

Cash glared. "This is messed up."

"I know but what the hell am I supposed to do about it?"

Cash swore. "There's got to be some way to let her know she's gonna be out of a space for her business in a few weeks."

Not only her business, but her home too. But his brothers didn't know that part. No one did. Save for him. Secretly he was already looking for new theaters and apartments for her. The latter was a lot easier to find than the former. But even if he did find her a new space, that didn't negate the fact that he was keeping information from her now.

"He can't say anything," Mal spoke up, grabbing the last bottle from Cash and opening it. "None of us can. Mr. Noll would sue us for everything we have, including Helping Homes. We can't allow that to happen."

Mal was more involved with their charity than he or Cash. His baby brother had a driving need to provide safety for those who needed it. He wasn't sure why. Mal had never shared what possessed him to fight so hard for others, but he was damn proud of his little brother.

"I know that, Mal, but we can't just leave Piper in the dark," Cash argued. "She's about to lose her business, and her landlord won't even give her a warning she's gonna be kicked out."

Mal's scowl increased, his grip tightening on his bottle. He muttered a dark curse, calling Donald a creative name Kell wholeheartedly agreed with.

"She's not losing her business," he reminded his brothers. "Just the building. And don't worry. I'm on the hunt for a new space."

Cash snorted. "Yeah, cause the metro area is

filled with vacant theater spaces that can accommodate aerialists."

"I said I'm on it, Cashel. If you really want to help Piper, then put some feelers out to your contacts." With Cash's charm, he tended to have the best client relationships. All the bigwigs with deep pockets loved his flattery and flirtatious ways.

Cash nodded, his anger deflating as he was presented with a task to help. "I can do that."

"Good." He nodded. "Let me worry about when Piper finds out and, in the meantime, we can do what we do best and find a space for someone who needs one."

Mal glanced at him, a question clear on his face even as his mouth remained closed.

"What is it, Malachy?" Because he knew his baby brother wanted to say something.

Mal worked his jaw, finally opening his mouth to ask. "Are you guys dating?"

The question shouldn't have surprised him. He did kiss her, twice, in his brothers' presence. To most people it would be obvious, but he knew Mal liked to have correct information on things directly told to him.

"Yes," he answered truthfully.

Mal's scowl deepened. "Makes things a bit more complicated, don't you think?"

"What do you think is going to happen when she finds out you're the agent selling this place and you knew all along?" Cash added.

Nothing good.

"Dammit, I know!" He ran a hand through his hair, sweat greasing his palm. He chugged the rest of his drink and tossed the bottle with more force than necessary into the dumpster. It clanged against the pile of broken shingles, thankfully not breaking.

"I know she'll be angry, and she'll have every right to be, but what the hell am I supposed to do? If I tell her, we could lose the charity, and if I don't..." He stared at his brothers, pleading with them to find a solution. "What do I do?"

Cash's gaze turned sympathetic. "I don't know, Kell."

Mal's scowl softened into a sad frown. He shrugged. His brothers were as adrift as he was. He had three weeks to find a solution to this problem, or he risked losing Piper forever.

She's going to leave anyway. Why delay the inevitable?

A dark cloud of impending doom washed over him. If his past was any indication, it was only a matter of time before Piper dropped him and found her real forever partner. What the hell was he doing? He knew this was going to end badly, but for some reason he couldn't stop what was happening. The thought of not spending this precious time he had left with Piper hurt worse than the inevitable heartbreak he knew was coming.

Not having Piper, having Piper and losing her,

both were torture. He might as well enjoy the bliss before the downfall. Or maybe he was just fooling himself into thinking this time would be different, even though, deep down, he knew it never would be. Guilt and fear collided in his gut. A deep wrenching pain no amount of antacid could fix. He had to face the facts. Piper was going to leave him one way or another. What he did with their time until then was up to him. He could run from it or…try and make enough warm memories to last through the dark lonely nights without her.

CHAPTER TWENTY

This can't be real.

Piper stared at herself in the full-length mirror in the condo bedroom. She didn't look like herself. Well, she did, but a fancy version of herself. Earlier today, a box had arrived with a message from Kell.

I'd be honored if you would join me for an evening of entertainment. I hope everything fits (I checked your sizes with Rachel). See you at six.
Kell

What possible entertainment could they enjoy while dressed like this? She stroked her hand down the dark blue gown, the tiny sparkling crystals bumping against her palm. The smooth silk was covered in them. The dress fell past her ankles, landing just above the floor and leaving her toes exposed in the sliver strappy heels that had also been in the box. It clung to her body perfectly, fitting like a glove. The bodice had some kind of boning structure, allowing her to wear it without a bra, which was nice. One arm was left bare while the other was covered in a flowy sheer lace with bits of crystals sparkling amongst the intricately woven threads.

She'd never worn anything so beautiful.

Or expensive.

She'd seen the designer's name, Vivienne Westwood. A fashionista she was not—Piper preferred comfort over brand names—but she knew enough to realize this dress must have cost Kell a fortune. Not to mention the beautiful earrings and necklaces that had also been included. The dark blue sapphires glistened against her skin, making the streaks of blue in her hair pop.

She'd done her best with her makeup and hair to match the elegance of the dress. A soft smoky eye paired with a deep rose lip. With her hair, she kept it simple. She had slicked it back and fashioned it into a soft low bun and added a bit of the fresh baby's breath that had come in the gorgeous bouquet of roses Kell sent along with the package.

"We're definitely not going to the movies." Not dressed like this.

A knock on the door interrupted her musings. She glanced at the clock on the wall. Six o'clock on the dot. Grabbing her small black clutch, she hurried to the front door and opened it. The air was knocked clean from her body at the sight she saw. Kell in a suit had been intoxicating. Kell in a tux was about to take her out.

"Wow!" she whispered.

That devilishly handsome grin curled his lips. "Hey, that's my line. You look absolutely beautiful, Piper. Does everything fit?"

She nodded, unable to form a single thought when he looked like he had literally just stepped out of her dreams.

"Excellent. Then are you ready to go?"

She blinked. Words finally coming back into her head. "Go where? Your note said a night of entertainment, but I gotta tell you, most of my experiences with entertainment don't require me to wear a dress that cost more than my rent." Or what her rent used to cost anyway.

"It's a surprise," Kell said, offering her his arm.

Slipping her arm thought his, she allowed him to escort her out of the building where her stomach took flight once again at what she saw waiting for them.

"Is that limo for us?"

"It is."

She glanced at him from the corner of her eye. "Really pulling out all the stops here. I thought men stopped trying to impress women once they gave it up."

She chuckled, but he didn't join in.

"Only immature little boys use devious tactics to manipulate others into getting what they want." He opened the limo door and offered her his hand. "I'm not trying to impress you, Piper. I'm giving you the things you deserve. And you, sweetheart, deserve the world."

She caught a hint of something in his eyes she couldn't decipher. What she could have done to deserve such expensive clothes and a limo ride, she had no idea, but if Kell wanted to spoil her, far be it from her to stop him. Tonight, she was living out her real-life fairy-tale dream.

Then why did she have a tingling of worry in her gut that something was wrong?

Pushing the thought away, she placed her hand in his and slid into the limo. The ride was smooth, despite the pothole-ridden city streets. She had no idea how the driver managed to miss every bump—maybe the limo was equipped with the world's best suspension system. Before she truly had time to enjoy the luxury of riding in a limo, the car pulled to a gentle stop.

"We're here," Kell said smiling.

"And where is here exactly?" He still hadn't told her what tonight's entertainment was.

Grinning like a kid on Christmas, Kell opened the door, stepped out and offered his hand. She allowed him to help her from the car, her breath leaving her lungs for a second time that night. Before her stood the brand-new Denver Opera House. Construction had been going on for over a year on the beautiful building.

"What are we doing here?" She frowned in confusion. "It's not supposed to be open for another month."

"To the public," Kell confirmed with a nod. "But tonight is a special preview performance for the angel investors."

She blinked, his words swirling around in her brain. "Angel investors? You're one of the angel investors for the Denver Opera House?"

"My family is. I told you my mother is a patron of the arts. Since she's out of the country and Cash and Mal aren't big on opera, I decided to take someone who I knew would appreciate the skill of the performers."

He led her toward the front doors, her mind still reeling from the shock. She loved opera, but she'd never been able to afford a live performance. The fact that she was going to be able to see a special preview… What was her life right now?!

They headed up the sleek stone stairs flanked by large Corinthian marble pillars. The tall double doors were open, doormen on either side, checking people in. The small crowd of people, all dressed in the most elegant dresses and tuxes Piper had ever seen, slowly made their way inside.

Kell handed a gold-foiled invitation to the doorman, who nodded before handing it back and motioning to a short white woman in a dark usher uniform.

"Your private box seats are ready for you, Mr.

Thorson. Should you need anything, Samantha will be at your service."

"Curtain is in ten minutes," Samantha said with a smile. "I can take you to your seats now if you would like?"

Kell nodded. "Thank you, Samantha, we would appreciate that."

"Box seats?" she whispered as they followed the usher. "You have private box seats?"

Kell just smiled with a small shrug.

Samantha led them up a set of stairs and down a short hall. The usher pulled back a large red velvet curtain to reveal a small balcony-sitting area with two very fancy and plush-looking chairs.

"There's a button on the wall just here," Samantha said, pointing. "Please don't hesitate to push it if you need anything. I'll come right away. Enjoy the show."

"Thank you," Kell said.

"Yes, thank you." Piper smiled at the young woman. For a split second, time suspended. She looked at Samantha in her pressed slacks and vest, white button-up underneath, and she was transported to a time not so long ago when she was the usher, picking up shifts to make ends meet between performance gigs. Now here she was in private box seats.

But I'm not really here.

Physically she was, but she had to remember the only reason she was getting this special treatment was because of the man beside her. She wasn't the rich fancy one. How long before someone here saw her for the fraud she was? An interloper, a pretender. At the theater, when he was in his jeans and flannel, she could pretend he was just a handyman. In the same economic class as her. But tonight was shattering her illusion. The man had money to burn. She wasn't sure how she felt about that. At least a sizeable portion of his wealth was going to fund the arts and help house those in need, according to him.

Maybe I should research him.

"Piper?"

She blinked, pulled out of her thoughts by the concern in Kell's voice.

"Are you okay?"

The genuine worry on his face calmed her racing thoughts. No. No surreptitiously online searching into his life. Kell had been nothing but honest with her. She was simply letting her past get the better of her. Kell wasn't Larry. She'd been careful this time. Tonight, she needed to let the past go and enjoy the present.

"I'm fine, just a little shocked at all…this."

"In a good way I hope."

He guided her to one of the chairs, waiting until she sat before taking his own.

"In a fantastic way. I love opera. I've never been able to see a performance live, but I've always dreamed of it."

"Then I am happy to make your dream come true."

The houselights dimmed, and a hush fell over the audience. Kell leaned forward to place a soft kiss on her lips. Her heart skipped several beats. As the curtain rose, she focused her attention on the stage, his words echoing in her mind. She couldn't help but wonder if this beautiful dream they were sharing would last, or if their differences were too vast an obstacle to overcome.

CHAPTER TWENTY-ONE

LAST NIGHT HAD been amazing. So amazing in fact that Piper had forgotten half the warm-up and gotten stuck trying to teach the most basic moves to her beginners' class. Her focus was shot. Hard to concentrate when her mind kept wandering back to the way Kell made her body sing last night after the opera. Which had been equally amazing. She'd never felt more like a princess in her life. A small giggle tried to claw its way up her throat, but she swallowed it back down. Time to keep it together. Class was nearly over.

As she walked the class through the cooldown stretches, she smiled. "Don't forget to drink lots of water. You all did great today."

The students thanked her as they packed up and headed out of the theater. Her gaze traveled up to the ceiling. Kell and his brothers were up there working on the roof today. She'd spent the night at his place, and he drove them back this morning. Spending the night in a comfy king-size bed had been a welcome change from her rickety old cot. She hoped to do it again soon. Not just for the bed—the company was the best part.

She let her smile grow, allowing the giggle to escape this time as she started to take down the slings. The teaching day was over. A good thing too, since she was starving. She wondered how Kell was doing. Would he finish soon, want to grab dinner?

Her phone beeped with a calendar alert. Picking it up from the spot on the floor where she'd placed it during class, she glanced at the notification. A heavy sigh left her. There were two weeks left on her lease and Donald hadn't sent her any paperwork on the renewal. She'd been hoping he'd send something soon, so she didn't have to actually talk to the man, but it was getting too close for comfort. She had to call him and get the ball rolling.

Bringing up her contacts, she pressed Donald's number and took a deep steadying breath.

"Yeah, what is it?"

What a delightful greeting. She shoved down her irritation.

"Hello, Mr. Noll. This is Piper Pitts."

"I know who the hell it is. Your name comes up on the damn screen."

Someone was in a cheery mood. This did not bode well for her, but time was of the essence, so she pushed on.

"I'm calling about my lease renewal. As you know, the lease is up in two weeks. I was wondering when you would be sending the new lease paperwork for me to sign?"

Silence filled the line.

"Mr. Noll?"

"I'm not," his gruff voice finally answered.

"Pardon?"

"I'm not sending the paperwork over to you."

Confused, she pressed her phone tighter to her ear. "Oh, um, did you want me to come to you and get it or—"

"No," he abruptly interrupted. "I'm not drawing up a new lease with you."

Now she was really confused. A prickle of apprehension tickled the back of her neck. Heart rate rising, she sought clarification. "I'm sorry, I don't understand."

Donald let loose a cruel bark of laughter. "Let me spell it out for you, sweetheart."

Gross. She nearly gagged at the endearment. It sounded beautiful coming from Kell, loving and precious. But Donald spat the word with a condescending sneer that felt slimy and mean.

"I'm not sending any new paperwork over because I'm not renewing your lease."

Her world slammed to a stop. Sweat gathered on her palms. The loud thump of her heart sounded like the drums of doom, leading her into a battle she had no hope of surviving.

"You're not renewing my—"

"I'm getting rid of the headache, once and for

all," he interrupted again, as if he hadn't just destroyed her with five simple words.

"Getting rid of…but I don't…all the fixes? You finally put work into…" Realization dawned on her. "Oh, you're fixing it up to sell, aren't you?"

His cruel laughter filled her ear. "You finally used the two brain cells you possess. Yeah, I'm selling the place."

Did Kell know? Did he know all his hard work making this place perfect for her would be going to someone else? Her anger at Donald grew twofold for lying to them both like this. Kell was going to be so upset. Why would a cheap man like Donald even waste his time with fixes? Why not sell the place "as is" and be done with it if he hated it so much?

"I don't understand why you're putting money into the fixes if you're just going to sell it?" Especially when she'd been asking for these fixes for years.

"My agent said it would fetch a higher price if we spruced it up a little. Since he's a licensed contractor, we worked all the repairs into his commission fee. I got a great deal, and I stand to make a mountain of money, so pack your bags, Ms. Pitts."

Wait…his real estate agent was also the contractor? As in…Kell? No, it couldn't be. He wouldn't. Kell was a good man, a kind soul. No way would he have been lying to her this whole time. She refused to believe he could do something so heartless.

"Your agent," she asked with a shaky voice, needing to know the truth. "What's his name?"

Donald barked out another cruel laugh. "You know the guy. He's been working around the place for the past six weeks. Kellen Thorson of Thorson Realty."

Her world turned dark. Piper sunk to the hard stage floor as her heart broke into a million piercing shards in her chest. She couldn't get enough air into her lungs as the panic clawed its way up her throat. She'd been wrong. So very, very wrong. The ridiculous notion she'd dismissed of Kell being a spy had been silly… He was so much worse.

Damn her for not googling him.

"You have two weeks to get all your junk out, Pitts."

Donald's harsh command raked along her spine, but it couldn't touch the pain tearing her soul apart.

"Two weeks isn't enough time," she said, managing to push the words past her dry throat.

"Yeah well, that's your problem not mine. We had a set end date for the lease. Legally I am under no obligation to renew it. Hell, I didn't even have to tell you I wasn't renewing it. Consider this a favor."

A favor? If she hadn't called and inquired, she knew 100 percent he would have shown up on the last day of the lease with eviction papers. Here he was trying to act like he was being generous? The man was a monster.

"Two weeks," he demanded again before the line went dead.

She sat on the stage, body overheating even as her soul felt frozen. How could he do this to her? Not Donald. That underhanded move she expected from the creep. But Kell? She thought they had something special. He understood her, cared for her…or so she thought. Maybe she was as naive as people said. Her initial instincts had been right. He'd been playing her from the beginning. Keeping her from seeing the obvious so she wouldn't do anything to hamper the sale. Not that she could anyway. She had no legal ground to stop Donald. It was his building.

What a fool she'd been.

It was the Larry situation all over again. When would she learn? What her grandparents had was an anomaly. The fairy-tale love she'd been chasing her whole life had done nothing but rip her heart into shreds. It was time to grow up and face the facts of the cold, cruel world.

Love was an illusion.

She sat on the cold stage floor, wondering what she was going to do, where she was going to go, when Kell's voice filled the air.

"There you are. We just finished up. Wanna grab some dinner? I promise these knuckleheads won't be joining us."

"Hey, that's hurtful, bro." Cash teased cheerfully.

She glanced up at the brothers. Normally the sight of Kell made her heart skip a beat. Not anymore. The cruel spike of betrayal twisted in her chest. She closed her eyes as tears leaked down her cheeks.

"Piper?"

She felt his presence by her side in seconds.

"What's wrong?"

His hand reached out, landing on her shoulder. The warm palm she normally took great comfort in burned her skin. A venomous touch, she now understood. Scooting back, she opened her eyes and glared at the face she once considered to be the most handsome she'd ever laid eyes on.

"Two weeks," she managed to growl out.

He shook his head, confusion pulling his brow down. "I don't understand."

"Two weeks," she repeated, the fire of betrayal burning away the sadness. "I just had a little chat with Donald about my lease renewal. The one that isn't happening because he's selling this place in two weeks."

His face went pale. She thought she heard Cash mutter something in the background, but she ignored it. All of her focus, all her ire, was reserved for the man before her who had broken her heart.

"How could you, Kell?" she whispered, unable to keep the pain from her voice. "How could you not tell me?"

"I wanted to, Piper, I swear." He held up his

hands, distress lining his face. "But Donald made me sign an NDA. If I told you anything about the sale, he could sue us into the ground. We'd lose everything, including Helping Homes. I couldn't risk the foundation. I had to..."

"Betray me," she finished for him.

He reared back as if she'd slapped him. "No... no. It wasn't like that."

"Then what was it like? Because from where I'm sitting, it looks exactly like that."

"Sweetheart, I—"

"Don't." She stood, glaring at him, allowing all the pain he'd caused her to seep into her eyes. "Don't ever call me that again. I was wrong about you, Kell. I thought we had something special, but in the end I'm the one to suffer. Maybe you are cursed after all."

She watched as something flicked in his eyes. The joyful spirit she'd always come to associate with this man splintered, resignation creeping into those once-happy eyes. A tiny ping of guilt wormed its way inside, but she shoved it down. She couldn't feel sorry for him when he was the one who knew all along and said nothing.

"Piper... I'm sorry... I..."

Cash came up behind his brother, gently grasping his arm and helping him stand. "Come on, man. Let's give her some space."

Cash gave her a sympathetic glance. She wondered how much his brothers knew. Probably everything. Did they laugh about her naivete behind her back? She felt so stupid!

Kell still stared at her as his brother tugged him away, a sheen of moisture filling those eyes that gazed at her with pain and regret. At least he felt bad. It meant he wasn't a complete monster. Mal glanced down as he passed by her. She followed his gaze to see her hand, fingers furiously fidgeting against her thigh. The anxiety filling her was about to burst into full-blown overwhelm.

"Do you need anything?" the usually silent brother asked.

She nodded over to the one sling still hanging on the stage. "I've got it."

He nodded, moving over to help Cash lead Kell out of the theater. Once they were gone, she walked over to the sling and slipped into the fabric. Placing the sling under her armpits, across her back, she started to spin. One toe on the ground, she used her other leg to gain momentum, spinning faster and faster. She let the tears fall, her movements flinging them against her body as she spun. A deep aching cry ripped from her throat as she lifted her legs, falling back.

The fabric caught on her hips as she spun upside down, but it still wasn't fast enough to calm her nerves. Tucking her knees in close on either side of the fabric, she made her body as small as possible to increase the spin. Finally, the panic started to ease. She stayed like that until the spin slowed, all the blood rushing to her head, tears sliding down into her hair.

"I am fortune's fool." She whispered the very apt Shakespeare quote into the empty theater.

Tilting back up, she placed her feet on the floor, slipped out of the sling and stood on the stage. The place she'd built her business on. The place that held countless performances over the years, helped hundreds of people discover a love of aerials. Not just a theater, but somewhere lifelong friendships were formed. A safe space for sensory seekers. This place wasn't just a building and a business. It was her heart.

And he'd destroyed it.

He'd destroyed all of it.

She thought he was her knight in shining armor, come to save the day, but she was wrong. Kell wasn't her prince. He was the frog, and she was a fool to believe they'd have a fairy-tale ending.

CHAPTER TWENTY-TWO

"THIS 'WOE IS ME' act is getting old, man."

Kell growled at Cash, pushing past his little brother to grab another beer from the fridge. They were all at his home after a long day of finishing up the roof at Star-Crossed Theater.

"You've been a real bummer on the job. Even Mal thinks so," Cash continued.

Mal grunted, grabbing the beer Kell handed him and shrugging noncommittedly. He thought about not handing a beer to Cash—his annoying little brother didn't deserve one—but they'd had a long workday and Cash was right. His mood the past week had been lower than the Mariana Trench.

"Sorry I'm not Sally Sunshine," he muttered, taking a deep swig of his beer. "But it's kind of hard to put on a happy face when I'm sweating my soul out working on that damned roof."

He was exceedingly glad that job was done. Not only because it had been hot as hell up there, but the roof repair had been the last part of the job. The repair job, that is. He still had to sell the place at the price Donald wanted for it.

"Oh, so the mopey mood has to do with heat intolerance and not the fact that you betrayed Piper?"

His hand tightened around the glass bottle. He hated that word. It was ugly and cruel and…true. He had betrayed Piper. But what choice did he have? He'd spent the past week doing his best to avoid her while he finished work on the roof. As much as he ached to see her, to try and explain again, he knew it was coming from a selfish place. The sight of him only caused her pain. Reminded her of his part in taking her business and home away. He'd already hurt her so much. It would be cruel of him to press the matter just to make himself feel better.

He knew things would eventually end. Story of his life. What he hadn't expected was how deep his feelings for Piper had become. He'd planned to have some fun and get out before he got hurt again. But he'd made a grave error. Now, not only was he hurting, but Piper was too. All because he thought he could have what he wanted for once.

What a fool he was.

"You know you're an idiot, right?" Cash said, flopping down on the couch.

Kell let out a heavy sigh, sinking into the armchair across from his brother. "Takes one to know one, baby brother."

"We're resorting to childish name-calling now?"

He shrugged. Glancing over to Mal, who sat

in an identical chair to his right, he lifted a hand. "You want to get in on this brother bashing?"

"I'm not bashing you," Cash insisted. "I'm trying to help you."

"I don't need help," he grumbled, picking at the label on his beer bottle. "I did my job and, in the process, hurt the woman I lo—hurt Piper. I'm a jerk. End of story."

The room fell silent. The weight of his actions pressed down on him.

"You're not a jerk," Cash said softly. "A jerk would imply that you did what you did out of malicious intent. You were stuck between a rock and a hard place. Should you have told Piper what was going on? Yes, but—"

"How?" he shouted, cutting Cash off. "How could I have told her about Donald's plans to sell without violating the NDA and opening us up to a lawsuit? Did you want me to risk Helping Homes? What would have happened then? What about all those people, those families that count on us to provide them with a place to live? A home? How can I put one person over hundreds in need?"

His heart pounded in his chest at the unfairness of it all. He'd tried. He'd tried so damn hard to find a solution where everyone won. But there hadn't been one.

"I couldn't do that to Helping Homes or you guys."

Because it wasn't just his charity. It was Cash's

and Mal's too. Damn Donald for telling her! All he'd needed was a few more days. He would have come up with a solution…probably. Now, it was too late. Piper was losing her theater, and he'd lost her.

The curse held strong.

Only if she meets the love of her life now.

He scowled, downing the rest of his beer. The thought of Piper with anyone else made his blood boil. He wanted her to be happy. She deserved happiness more than anyone in the entire world. But for the first time in a long time, he wanted to be that someone. He wanted to be the one to make her happy, to hear her laughter, to hold her in the dark of the night.

I lost that right.

And he had no clue how to earn it back.

"We could have helped you find a way to tell her," Cash said. "You don't always have to take on every problem yourself, Kellen."

"I don't do that—"

"You do," Cash insisted.

He glanced over to Mal for confirmation.

"You always have." Mal nodded.

His inner voice agreed with his brothers and was just as annoying. Sinking back into his chair, he scowled at the two. "Yeah, well, I'm the oldest. It's my job to take care of you two knuckleheads."

"Maybe when we were kids and Mom and Dad left you in charge, but we're adults, Kell. We can make our own decisions. Help out. You don't have to protect us anymore. We could have helped you find a solution."

"I don't see how," he grumbled. "The clause in the contract was airtight."

"It was a ridiculous clause," Mal muttered, finishing off his beer.

He agreed, but they'd all read it and signed it. It hadn't seemed so bad. Until he met Piper and realized the gravity of what he'd just done. He'd signed his soul away to the devil. A bit dramatic, but it was how he felt right now.

"But," Mal continued. "I understand why you stayed silent. You were following the rules and protecting the people who need us. You did the right thing by them."

The youngest of the Thorson brothers was a strict rule follower. Kell knew rules made Mal feel safe, in control. Still, knowing he did the right thing did nothing to ease the raw, tearing pain ripping his soul to shreds. If it had been right, why did he feel so wrong?

"Sometimes the right thing is the wrong thing," Cash said.

Mal frowned. "That doesn't make any sense."

None of this made sense. It was all one giant mess with no discernible solution. Like the trolley problem. Do you save the one person or the five? Either way, someone is going to be hurt so can there really be any solution that is "right" or is the question, in itself, always wrong?

Dammit. He needed another beer.

He made his way to the fridge, calling over his shoulder. "You guys want another beer?"

"Are we wallowing?" Cash asked. "'Cause beer isn't the drink of a pity party. That's a job for tequila. Of course, last time we did tequila shots you were praising the porcelain gods the next day, so maybe you should stick to something milder for your delicate system."

His little brother was riding his last nerve. Cash turned everything into a joke. Nothing about this situation was funny.

"I'm not wallowing." He grabbed three beers, slamming the fridge door shut with more force than necessary as he glared at Cash. "I'm just… upset. This whole situation is messed up and I thought…"

Making his way back to the living room, he passed his brothers their drinks and sunk back into his chair.

"I don't know why I thought I could break the stupid curse," he muttered, twisting off the cap and drinking deeply.

"Curse?" Mal frowned.

"You gotta be freaking kidding me." Cash pointed the neck of his beer bottle at Kell. "Do you still believe that ridiculous 'curse' notion?"

"What curse?" Mal said, scooting forward on his chair.

Cash pointed to Kell "Fool over here got it into his head that he's cursed by love. That every woman he dates breaks up with him then immediately finds her one true love. It's why he stopped serious relationships a few years back."

He snorted, lifting his beer bottle as he spoke. "You're one to talk, Mr. New Girlfriend Every Two Weeks."

"Hey." Cash held up a hand. "That's different and we're talking about you, not me. You're not cursed."

"I am," he insisted.

"Curses aren't real," Mal replied.

Sure as hell felt real. He'd opened his heart again only for the universe to crush it.

"Let's look at the facts," Cash said, sitting forward and placing his beer on the coffee table. He held up a hand and started counting off on his fingers. "You got hired for a job to fix up and sell the theater, but you couldn't tell the current owner about the sale for risk of losing Helping Homes."

"Yeah, we know all this, Cash."

"But," Cash continued, holding up another finger. "Once you met the tenant, Piper, you started falling for her and felt guilty so you tried to come up with a way to tell her, but Donald did it before you could. Now she's rightfully mad at you and you guys broke up, leading you to think the curse worked its magic again."

His jaw clenched at the cavalier way Cash pointed it out. "Yeah, your point?"

"If the curse is real, as you so often like to say, then the next person Piper is with will be her one true love."

And he would like to knock whoever the person would be into the stratosphere. Whoever they were, they better treat her like the goddess she was, or they'd have to answer to him.

"So be that guy," Cash finished, sitting back with a smug smile.

"Huh?"

"Be the next person Piper is with. Go to her, Apologize, find a way to earn back her trust and live happily ever after or whatever."

He barked out a laugh of disbelief. Of course Cash would think it would be that easy.

"Are you kidding? You heard what she said. I doubt she ever wants to talk to me again. I ruined her life. Her studio might go under, thanks to me."

"Technically it's Donald's fault," Mal pointed out. "Not yours."

"I don't think she sees it that way." He sure as hell felt responsible for it.

"She's had some time to think." Cash shrugged. "Maybe now she'll be able to realize what a hard position you were in. She's a good person, she'll understand. Go apologize again."

"And what about the theater? Her business? She's going to be kicked out in a week. What am I supposed to do about that?"

Mal shared a look with Cash. "Help her find a new one? Isn't that our job?"

It was, but she loved that theater. He saw it every day. The way her face lit up when she stepped onto the stage. It wasn't just a building to her. It was her heart and soul. Her home. Literally at times. He couldn't allow Donald to sell it off to some random person. No one would love that place like Piper because no one loved like Piper. She loved with her entire being. He knew that because—

"I love her," he whispered into the room. And she loved him. Or she had before he screwed everything up. His only hope was that their love still burned, an ember he could fan back into flames if he apologized and made amends.

"Yeah, man, we know." Cash grinned. "What are you going to do about it?"

He was going to show this damned curse it didn't rule his life anymore. He was going to show Donald he couldn't push people around. He was going to win back the love of his life and give her everything she deserves and more.

He stood, determination set as he stared at his brothers. "I'm going to see a man about a theater."

CHAPTER TWENTY-THREE

AS IF HER life couldn't get any worse, the food delivery guy forgot her crab wontons. Piper grumbled as she dug through the bag, but sadly her wontons did not appear.

"Perfect. Just the perfect end to a disastrous week."

"What's that, babe?" Rachel asked from her seat on the couch.

"They forgot my wontons," she muttered as she reclaimed her seat next to Rachel.

Her best friend had come into the theater that fateful night to grab her yoga mat she'd forgotten, and found Piper sobbing in the sling. After a good fifteen minutes crying in her arms, Piper finally found the words to tell Rachel everything that had happened. She told her about Donald selling the place and how Kell knew since he was the real estate agent. She hadn't even known he *was* a real estate agent.

You think you know a person.

After talking Rachel down from sending Donald a glitter bomb, Piper confessed she had no idea what to do next. Every night this week she'd come over to Rachel's place after classes so they could brainstorm next plans.

It wasn't going well.

Much like her life lately.

"What did I do to anger the universe? Why is it taking a big dump all over my life?" She flopped back against the couch, misery weighing her down.

"Hun, you know I love you, but this 'woe is me' shtick has got to go soon. This isn't like you."

Jaw dropping wide, she stared at her supposed best friend. "Well, excuse me. I'm not sure who I'm supposed to be in times like this."

Rachel grabbed her cashew chicken, opened the carton and plucked a piece of meat with her chopsticks. "Times like these?"

"Yeah, I've never had my livelihood ripped right out from under me while also being betrayed by the man I lo—" She cut herself off.

"The man you…" Rachel raised an eyebrow.

"Nothing," she muttered into her lo mein, digging in.

She would not say the L word. Not about Kell. She didn't love him. She couldn't, or this pain she was feeling would destroy her. It was already ripping her apart regardless, but saying it out loud after what he did… She feared that would be her end.

"Look," Rachel said, putting down her food and

swiveling on the couch so she was facing Piper. "Donald is the jerkiest jerk in jerk town."

"He's the mayor of jerk town," she growled.

"The president of jerk town." Rachel smiled.

They looked at each other and at the same time said, "The king of jerk town!"

A fit of laughter followed. It felt nice to laugh again. She hated this sick feeling of dread and sadness lodged in her chest the past week. Donald's actions—those she should have seen coming. She was angry, but not surprised her scummy landlord pulled a stunt like this. If it was just losing the theater, she'd still be distraught, but she could manage. But Kell's betrayal…

That was a wound she feared she may never recover from.

"Okay, so we've determined Donald is a jerk," Rachel said with a nod. "And this past week searching through the rental listings has gotten us zero results for a new place for the studio."

"Don't remind me," she groaned, shoveling another chopstick full of noodles into her mouth.

She had wished on a shooting star the night before she found the listing for Star-Crossed Theater. Fate had been in her favor then. Now, not so much. There weren't many theaters equipped to handle aerial rigging. A dance studio wouldn't work because the ceilings weren't high enough and she'd have to pay for structural support of the aerial equipment. She couldn't afford that.

"There's still time to send him a glitter bomb." Rachel gave her a look. "An innocent looking package sent to his doorstep and when he opens it up...*bam*, face full of glitter!"

Piper still couldn't believe that there were companies who offered that service. As much as she loved the idea of Donald's grumpy face being covered in glitter for all eternity—because that's how long glitter stayed on you, she should know, she was a performer—she shook her head.

"No. At least not yet. I still have one more week to figure things out. Who knows, maybe a miracle will happen, and he'll change his mind about selling." She had a better chance of winning the lottery and she didn't even play. "Besides, he would know it's me and kick me out even sooner. Half of my stuff is still in the storage room."

That night Rachel found her sobbing, she'd also confessed about her living arrangements, staying at the theater after Larry screwed her over, Kell offering his family condo. Rachel had wanted to trash the place—in furious defense of her—but Piper just wanted to get her stuff and never set eyes on the place again. What she first assumed was kindness, she now wondered if his "generosity" had simply been a way to assuage his guilt. She'd been crashing at a cheap motel the past week. Not smart for her budget, but she couldn't be in that condo without thinking about Kell. Wondering how she'd been so foolish, missed all the signs.

The pain and embarrassment swirled inside her. A hurricane threatening to destroy what little hope she had left.

Rachel's eyes narrowed. "Yeah, about that. I'm still mad you didn't tell me about Larry leaving you homeless."

She searched very intently for a snow pea in her food, avoiding her best friend's glare.

"I can't believe you decided living at the theater was better than living with me. You know Naya would be cool with it."

"I know." Naya, who was currently at her bartending job, truly was the sweetest woman ever. She'd even spent her one night off last night helping Piper scour the internet for building rentals. "But come on, Rachel, where would I fit in here, huh? There's barely enough room for you two."

"We could make it work."

"You're both very sweet, but no. Thankfully I have a few leads on some room rentals so at least that part of my life seems to be falling into place."

She didn't particularly like living with roommates, but beggars couldn't be choosers. She'd just have to deal with the overstimulation and discomfort of living with others until she got her life sorted out.

"I'm glad to hear that. One problem down, one to go."

Too bad this one looked insurmountable. Piper hadn't even told her students yet. What could she tell them? She had nowhere to teach classes next week. No studio, no theater. She'd have to temporarily close her business. How was she supposed to come up with the funds for a new lease if she wasn't making money teaching classes?

"We've looked everywhere," she moaned into her take-out box. "There's nothing out there that can handle the needs of an aerial studio."

"Maybe you should see if you can ask someone to help?" Rachel suggested. "Someone who has more experience with this stuff than me and Naya. Someone…in real estate?"

She must have passed out due to the stress because Rachel did not just suggest she ask Kell, the man who betrayed her and broke her heart, for help.

"Are you serious right now?" She stared at Rachel, heart racing. "After what he did to me?"

Putting down her food, Rachel held up a hand. "Hear me out. I know what Kell did was crappy and I plan to make him suffer for it. Don't worry, a glitter bomb is already heading his way—"

"Rachel, no!" She was furious at Kell, but the last thing his handsome face needed was glitter. It would only bring more attention to it.

"Already done, hun. I know he hurt you, but you have to admit the guy was stuck in a very awful position. Didn't he say Donald made him sign an NDA and if he told you about the sale Donald could sue him for everything, including that charity he runs with his brothers?"

She'd told her best friend too much. Rachel wasn't supposed to point out the logic in this situation. She was supposed to be on Piper's side and contemplate posting bogus bad reviews on his business site. Not that she ever would, but she thought about it.

"I bet it killed him not to tell you, Piper, but would you really want him to be the type of person who risked a charity that helps house people in need?"

No. She wouldn't feel the same way about him if he tossed aside others for his own desires. One of the reasons she cared for Kell so much was his generous heart. He was always helping people, herself included. It was Kell who helped sell out their show. Kell who fixed every broken item in the theater even if it wasn't on Donald's list. He would never abandon others for selfish reasons.

"Okay," she admitted. "Maybe he was in a tough spot, but I'm not ready to forgive him."

"Good. Don't." Rachel nodded. "Make the man grovel a little, but don't cut him off completely."

"Not sure that's up to me anymore."

She'd said some awful things to him the night she found out about the sale. Cruel, hurtful things. Her anger had overtaken common sense, mouth running, spewing all the pain she felt back at him. The agonized look in his eyes when she told him he was cursed haunted her in the dark of the night. That hadn't been fair. She'd been lashing out, hoping to wound him, make him feel an ounce of the betrayal she felt. Sadly, it looked as though it worked. The past week he'd been very careful not to cross her path while working at the theater.

"What? 'Cause you had a fight? Ha!" Rachel shrugged off her worries. "The man is head over heels in love with you. Guarantee you send one text, and he'll come running."

She blinked in surprise. "He's not in love with me. He doesn't believe in love. He thinks he's cursed. I was trying to prove otherwise but then…" Everything had blown up in their faces. Much like Rachel's glitter bombs.

"Babe, that man looks at you like you hung the moon and the stars. He is so far gone for you he doesn't know what to do. If he wasn't, would he have been so torn about telling you? Would he be as careful as he is not to upset you by coming into your space while you're angry at him? Would he be texting your best friend all week asking if you're okay?"

"He's doing what?" She pounced for Rachel's phone sitting on the coffee table. "Let me see."

"Ah ah, no." Rachel scooped up her phone before Piper could reach it. "He didn't want to upset you anymore, but he was worried about you. He's been checking in. Nothing creepy or invasive, just—"

Rachel's phone pinged. She glanced at it, a smile curling her lips as she chuckled.

"Speak of the devil. Looks like he got my present."

"Rachel, no!"

Lunging across the couch, she snatched the phone from her best friend's hand. Her heart skipped a beat at what she saw. Kell's face, covered in glitter, a resigned sparkly expression with text underneath saying *I deserve this*. A sob of laughter left her. Her finger scrolled up through the conversation. Kell apologizing, Rachel calling him some very creative names. Kell checking to make sure she was okay. Every day. Every day since that night he'd checked on her. Every day he'd lamented his inaction.

She clutched the phone to her chest, the truth of their horrible situation sinking in.

"Damn you, Donald."

Rachel was right. Kell's hands had been tied. She wouldn't have respected him anymore if he threw away Helping Hands for her. He did the right thing, even if it bit her on the butt in the end.

"I love him," she whispered.

"I know, babe." Rachel pulled her into a warm hug. "And I know this situation sucks, but maybe you could talk to him? Find a way to work all this out? But still, make him grovel. I want you to be happy, but the man needs to suffer a little more."

She laughed through her tears, clutching her best

friend tight. "You're the best and he's never going to get all that glitter off."

"I know." Rachel let out an evil snicker. "Serves him right."

She let out a wobbly breath. "Okay, I'll text him. Later. I'm not ready tonight."

"Totally get it. Now what do you say we pop this food in the fridge and head to the bar so my beautiful girlfriend can get us some celebratory drinks."

"What are we celebrating?"

"The possibilities of the future. You know what they say, always look on the bright side of life."

Her future was still too hazy for Piper to look on the bright side, but tonight had brought out some revelations and she had nothing but possibilities ahead of her. Thc drcad of the past week started to melt away as she realized she had more help on her side than she first thought. Kell hadn't lied and abandoned her. He still cared. She clung on to that knowledge with the last bit of hope she had left in her heart. As for what the future held…time would tell.

CHAPTER TWENTY-FOUR

Hey, can we talk?

PIPER STARED AT the unsent text on her phone. It had been there for two days. She kept typing and deleting, but had yet to drum up the courage to hit Send. Logically she knew Kell cared for her, and he hadn't kept silent about the sale of Star-Crossed Theater out of ill intent. His hands had been legally tied. She got that. But the scared little part of her deep inside, that part that had been hurt by others before, tricked and lied to, was still wary.

At least the other parts of her life seemed to be heading down a better path. She'd met her future roommates yesterday and signed a six-month lease. She would be sharing a house with two go-go dancers and a drag queen whose entire wardrobe she wanted to borrow. She still hadn't found a new studio, but it was the middle of summer. Colorado had a few more good weather months, and she'd looked into having the rest of the summer classes outside at Wash Park with her portable rigs.

Not the ideal situation, but it meant that she

wouldn't have to close her aerial studio right away. It gave her a few more months to find a place. She would make it work. Now if only she could make this thing with Kell work. But that would require actually talking to the man.

She slipped her phone back into her pocket, message unsent.

"Coffee for Piper." The barista's voice rang out in the small coffee shop.

"That's me, thank you."

She rushed to the counter to grab the sweet elixir of life. The worst part about living in a tiny motel room was not having space for her coffee setup. Thankfully the locally owned shop just a block away had delicious, affordable coffee. She might be on a tight budget, but she could not live without her coffee. At least she'd be able to make it at home again when she moved into the house next week.

Sipping her sweet caffeine fix, she headed out of the shop, back to the theater. The bright summer sun shone down on her, heating her body, making her second-guess not getting her coffee iced. As she walked up to the theater her heart stopped. The large red-and-white for-sale sign had been taken down.

Donald just put it up a few days ago. Had the theater already sold? She wasn't surprised. It was a beautiful building with so much potential. Anyone would be lucky to own this place. She knew he was kicking her out at the end of this week when her lease was up, but secretly she'd hoped he wouldn't be able to sell it right away. Or at all. Selfishly she'd dreamt of Donald coming back to her on his knees, begging to renew her lease. She'd agree, at a discounted rate of course.

But it appeared her dreams were just that. Based on the lack of sign, someone had bought the Star-Crossed Theater. Quickly too. Could someone buy a building that fast? Weren't inspections needed? Loan approvals?

Unless someone paid cash.

Her heart broke thinking of some rich jerk buying this place to turn it into a trendy nightclub or flip it for a profit. It wasn't fair. She loved this theater, spent years putting soul and art into its bones. And now some rich punk was going to do who-knew-what with it.

Swiping away an angry tear, she marched up the front steps into the building. She pulled out her keys and inserted them into the lock, discovering it was already unlocked. Uh oh. She'd locked up before she left, she knew it. Had Donald already given keys to the new owner? That scumbag! She still had five days left on her lease. This was still her place for one hundred and twenty more hours.

Flinging the door open, she stormed inside. The place was empty. As far as she could tell, no one was in the foyer. The slight sound of movement from beyond sounded in the air. Something being moved on stage. Her mood darkened. Someone was in the theater. She started forward, wishing she had the Wiffle Ball bat. Not that she would attack the new owner—if that was who was in here—but this was still her building, dammit, and she had the right to be angry that someone invaded her space.

With a soft tread, she made her way to the doors that led to audience seating. As quietly as possible, she opened the door and peeked her head through. A quick scan of the audience revealed nothing. No one in the seats. As she glanced to the stage, she saw a spotlight on center stage illuminating the dark brown wooden podium they used when people booked the theater for presentations or graduation ceremonies.

"What in the world?" she whispered.

Cautiously making her way inside, she puzzled at what could be going on. She certainly hadn't put the podium on the stage or messed with the lights. No one had keys to the light room except for her. And Donald—as the owner he had the master keys to everything. Why in the world would Donald come in here and set up a podium with a spotlight?

Her heart raced as horrible scenarios crept up in her mind. It would be just like Donald to set up some sick display letting her know the place had been sold. She couldn't see what was on the podium, but she wouldn't put it past him to leave a taunting letter informing her that someone bought the theater. The man was cruel like that.

Carefully making her way up to the stage, she put her coffee down and hopped onstage. Her nerves raced the closer she got to the podium, fingers frantically tapping on her thighs as overwhelm threatened to consume her. Taking a deep, steadying breath, she moved around the podium so she could see if there was anything on it.

There was.

Her heart cracked as she spied the paper lying on the dark wood surface with bold letters declaring it the deed for the Star-Crossed Theater. Her eyes closed as pain filled her chest. One warm tear leaked out, sliding down her cheek. She knew it was coming. Knew someone would buy the theater, but it still broke her heart to lose this place she loved so much. The place that had been a part of her life for the last six years. The place she built her business, taught students, made friends. It was more than just a building. It was a piece of her heart. And now it belonged to someone else.

Opening her eyes, she glanced over the paperwork, a name jumping out at her. Confused, she picked up the deed and read it again. The name didn't change. Disbelief filled her as she tried to understand what it meant. But it didn't make sense. How could it?

"What in the world?" she muttered, reading over the paper again. "This can't be real."

"It's real," a voice from backstage called.

Letting out a small shriek, Piper whirled around,

heart in her throat at the unexpected sound. A man stepped out from the shadows. A man who made her heart race and break all at the same time.

"Dammit, Kell! What did I tell you about sneaking up on me like that?"

A small grin tugged at the corner of his lips. "Sorry, didn't meant to scare you. At least you didn't have a bat with you this time."

He chuckled. She didn't join in, but the edge of her lips quivered as she fought a smile. The sight of him, after so many days of not seeing him, made her heart ache and yearn. She wanted to run to him, throw her arms around him and kiss him until neither of them could breathe again. But first she needed answers. And as Rachel pointed out, the man should grovel a little.

"What's going on?" she asked, holding up the deed. The deed that had her name on the owner's line.

How?

Kell sighed, his smile slipping. "I know what I did was wrong. I am so sorry I kept news about the sale from you, Piper. I wanted to tell you so much, but I couldn't. The NDA was unbreakable. I swear if I could have told you without risking Helping Homes I would have. I am so damn sorry, you have to believe me."

She did. As angry and betrayed as she felt, she understood the position Kell had been in.

"I know," she said softly. "It was an awful clause

that I should have expected from Donald, and it wasn't fair of him to put you in that situation. I was just collateral damage."

"No, sweetheart, no." He rushed to her side, his hands reaching out to hold her, but he paused. "This is all on me. I'm just as much to blame as Donald. I should have found a way to tell you without breaking the contract. There's always a way, and it's my fault for not discovering it. I hurt you and it's the very last thing in this world I ever wanted to do. I'm sorry, Piper."

She nodded, tears streaming down her cheeks. His apology didn't take away the pain of his betrayal, but it did soothe the lingering anger in her chest, melting it away.

Kell reached up and wiped away her tears with his thumbs, cupping her face in his hands. "I'm so sorry. I was so focused on trying to find a way to tell you Donald was selling the place I completely missed the solution to the problem."

"Solution?"

He grinned, nodding to the deed in her hand. "The sale."

She shook her head, still cradled in his palms. "But I don't understand. I didn't buy the theater. I can't buy the theater."

She knew Donald, and the guy was probably asking way over what this building was worth. Not that she wouldn't pay it if she had the money. She'd pay anything to own this theater, if only she could.

"But I can," Kell said. "And I did. For you."

Her eyes widened at his confession. "You bought a theater for me?"

Wait until she told Rachel. This went way beyond groveling.

He nodded. "I can't believe I didn't see it before. It was right there. Donald was selling the place, you deserved to have it, I have the money and I didn't even have to pay my own commission. It's a win all around."

She pulled away, shaking her head. "No, no. You can't buy me a theater. It's too much!"

"It's not enough," he insisted. "It will never be enough to make up for my actions. If it makes it easier to accept, we can work out a deal. My family always needs spaces for our charity galas. Take the theater and let us host our fundraising events here."

That sounded doable. Plus, if she let the Thorson family have events here, all their rich friends would see her aerial company information and maybe some of them would become donors or whatever rich people did. Still, she couldn't wrap her head around the fact that he actually bought the place for her. "Who buys someone a theater? This is ridiculous, it's too much, it's…it's…"

"It's true love," Kell said.

Her sputtering stopped. She stared, jaw wide as the L word dropped from his lips.

"You…don't believe in true love."

"I didn't," he agreed. "Until you came along,

insisting you'd be the one to break the curse. The curse we both know is silly, but I clung to it so hard. I was afraid of getting my heart broken again. I couldn't understand what was wrong with me. Why I wasn't enough for someone to stay forever. And then I realized. It wasn't me. It was that I hadn't found you yet."

A sob caught in her throat. He gently grasped her hands in his, pulling her close.

"Piper. All my life I thought I wasn't enough, but it turns out none of my past relationships worked out because they weren't with you. You are the one I'm supposed to be with. Call it fate or fairy-tale magic or whatever. All I know is I love you, with every ounce of breath I have inside me. I want to spend the rest of my life making sure you get every moment of happiness and joy you deserve and, sweetheart, you deserve it all."

More tears streamed down her face. At this point she'd be dehydrated if she didn't get some water soon.

"Kell," she whispered between shuddering breaths. "I love you too. You deserve all the happiness and joy too, even when you think you don't. I should refuse a gift as lavish as an entire building, but Rachel did say to make you grovel and I think as far as grand gestures go, this one takes the cake."

He laughed. "I can see her saying that. I'll be

picking glitter out of my hair for years, thanks to her."

She laughed along with him, spying a hint of glittery gold in his dark eyebrows.

"I love you, Kell."

"I love you too, Piper."

He pulled her into his arms, staring down at her with a wolfish smile. "You know, someone once told me that a curse can be broken by true love's kiss. Wanna give it a shot?"

She grinned. "Sounds like that person is pretty smart."

"She is, and talented, beautiful, charming, and now, a theater owner."

She closed her eyes, lifting on her toes as he pressed their lips together. Her heart sang at the taste of him. A taste she had feared she might never get to experience again.

Life had a funny way of giving you exactly what you wanted in a way you didn't know you needed. She finally had the theater, and in her name. Her aerial studio was secure and, best of all, her heart would be forever loved.

This first act of life had been a wild ride for sure. She couldn't wait for act two.

EPILOGUE

Three months later

"PIPER, DARLING, THAT WAS the most successful benefit we have ever had. You're amazing."

Piper smiled at Mrs. Thorson. They had just finished the first fundraising gala held at the Star-Crossed Theater, benefiting a new charity scholarship the Thorson family was starting for neurodivergent youth and adults interested in aerial arts. It had been Kell's idea, but she'd helped plan the event.

"Thank you, Mrs. Thorson, but Kell did most of the work."

"I've told you a thousand times to call me Jeanie, dear. And I know it was my son's idea, but the magic of the night was thanks to you and your students. My heart was racing with every drop and spin. Now I must go, but I'll see you this weekend at dinner?"

She still couldn't believe she now had monthly dinners at the Thorson mansion.

Her life had changed so much in the past few

months. Classes were full to the brim, the theater was running smoothly for the first time ever, she no longer had to deal with Donald the scumbag because she finally owned this place.

But best of all was Kell. After they'd made up, he'd begged her to come live with him. Thankfully her soon-to-be new roommates let her out of her lease since one of them had a sibling in need of a room to rent ASAP.

The Thorson Foundation had three more fund-raising galas on the schedule for the year. It worked out nicely as Piper could work the galas in between aerial shows. And displaying flyers for upcoming shows in the lobby, in full view of the gala attendees, was destined to work wonders for ticket sales if tonight was any indication. They'd nearly sold out next month's performance already.

Piper waved as Jeanie left the building. Then, with a happy sigh, she turned around and headed back into the theater to shut the lights off. As she glanced at the stage, a smile curved her lips. There, in the middle of the stage, sitting in a low sling was the man who made all her dreams come true. Kell.

"Does this mean you're ready for another lesson?" she asked, making her way up the stairs onto the stage.

"Not a chance," Kell chuckled. "I just needed to get you on stage so I could do this."

"Do what—"

A gasp left her as Kell slid from the sling onto

one knee. He reached into his tux pocket and pulled out a small black box.

"Piper Pitts, you are the most amazing person I have ever had the privilege of knowing. You have the kindest heart, the most optimistic outlook, and I'm still not convinced you aren't actually a goddess."

She laughed out a sob as tears of happiness started to leak from her eyes.

"I once thought I was cursed by love, but you showed me it wasn't a curse at all. I was just waiting for you. My one true love. You've turned me into a sappy romantic and I wouldn't have it any other way. I want to spend the rest of my life falling in love with you each and every day. Will you do me the honor of taking me as your husband?"

"Yes!"

Joy and excitement overwhelmed her. She knelt, throwing her arms around him. The move caught him off-balance and they both fell into the sling. Kell chuckled as he settled them into the fabric. They swayed, embracing as the stage lights filtered through the pink material, casting them in a rosy glow.

"We're the real deal, Piper." Kell kissed her softly, slipping the silver ring with a sparking sapphire on to her finger.

"See?" She grinned. "I told you I was right about happily-ever-afters. And I'm also right about you trying aerials again. See how fun this is?" She pushed off with her foot, spinning them slightly.

He laughed. "Yes to the fairy-tale ending. No to breaking my neck falling out of this thing." A wicked spark of heat entered his eyes. "But I can think of other things we could try in it."

She giggled in delight as his hands went to her zipper. Life had a funny way of giving you the thing you wanted in the most unexpected way. She thought Kell had been all wrong for her, but in the end, he was exactly who she needed. No one knew what the future would hold. All she knew was as long as they were together, things would work out because true love conquers all.

* * * * *

Look out for the next story in the
Love Under Construction trilogy
Coming soon!

And if you enjoyed this story, check out these
other great reads from Mariah Ankenman

Cinderella's Bargain with the Billionaire
Accidently Dating the Enemy

All available now!